MOUNTAIN OF ASHES

A COSMIC LOVE STORY

ALSO BY JOHN REED

Van Gogh's Gypsy
Dark Forest
Thirteen Mountain
Shadow White as Stone
The Kingfisher's Call
Assume the Position

Mountain of Ashes

A Labyrinth of Souls Novel

BY

John Reed

ShadowSpinners Press

Cover art by Josephe Vandel.
Book design by Matthew Lowes.

ShadowSpinners Press
shadowspinnerspress.com

Typeset in
Minion Pro by Robert Slimbach
and IM FELL Double Pica by Igino Marini.
The Fell Types are digitally reproduced
by Igino Marini, www.iginomarini.com.

Learn more about
the Labyrinth of Souls game at
matthewlowes.com/games.

To Stephen Vessels for shepherding me along unfamiliar paths, and for his advice: listen to the chrome lizards.

"What cosmic currents can pass through the holding of hands and the communication of bodies of two beings in love!"

—Dr. Robert Muller

Editor's Preface

Dungeon Solitaire: Labyrinth of Souls is a fantasy game for tarot cards, written by Matthew Lowes and Illustrated by Josephe Vandel. In the game you defeat monsters, disarm traps, open doors, and explore mazes as you delve the depths of a dangerous dungeon. Along the way you collect treasure and magic items, gain skills, and gather companions.

Now ShadowSpinners Press is publishing this and other stand-alone novels inspired by the game. Each *Labyrinth of Souls* novel features a journey into a unique vision of the underworld.

The Labyrinth of Souls is more than an ancient ruin filled with monsters, trapped treasure, and the lost tombs of bygone kings. It is a manifestation of a mythic underworld, existing at a crossroads between people and cultures, between time and space, between the physical world and the deepest reaches of the psyche. It is a dark mirror held up to human experience, in which you may find your dreams … or your doom. Entrances to this realm can appear in any time period, in any location. There are innumerable reasons why a person may enter, but it is a place antagonistic to those who do, a place where monsters dwell, with obstacles and illusions to waylay adventurers, and whose very walls can be a force of corruption. It is a haunted place, ever at the edge of sanity.

MOUNTAIN OF ASHES

Chapter One

A hundred feet down the cliff, Matt Thanos decided he didn't want to die.

He let go of the Harley's handlebars and spread his arms, fingers clutching at the air. The bike executed a lazy turn below him, tires to the sky. Matt plummeted, feet above his head.

A flash of silver in the sun: his wife Emily's funeral urn tumbled through the air beside him. Images of her filled his mind. Dark hair swirling around her face, the bottomless blue of her eyes. The sheen of black satin hugging her loins. In moments he would be dead. Those memories—and Emily—would be gone forever. He arched his back, body rigid—fighting gravity. Mist drifted around him, chilling his skin. His gloved fingers brushed the urn. Distant sounds of water grew to a roar. An icy shock overwhelmed his senses as he plunged into a river. The torrent pulled him under and swept him down the canyon.

And then, stillness. The river had thrown him aside.

He opened his eyes and waited for pain. None came. All he could see was darkness.

He must be dead.

He gasped for breath; chills shook his body. His motorcycle leathers were soaked. He sat up, pulled off his gloves and flexed his arms. No broken bones—he didn't feel any injuries. He should be dead. He had fallen hundreds of feet, been sucked into an underground torrent and tossed onto a rocky bank. But he was breathing. And he wasn't dead.

Endless fighting with his wife and her mother had finally driven him insane. The pills the doctors had given him had only made things worse. That was it: drug-induced madness—he was imagining this. Crazy or not, he couldn't just lie here on the rocks. He was alive—with his memories of Emily.

He felt around in the darkness. Cold, rough stone. He crawled away from the water, boot toes scraping against rock, and bumped his head on an unseen wall. He stood and reached up, found only empty space above him. Stumbled to his knees, got back up and felt his way along the wall, sliding his feet on the stone, fighting to control the growing feeling of panic. Trapped in utter darkness. He convulsed, struggling to breathe.

The water's roar echoed off cavernous stone, deep and hollow as a cathedral. The sound grew louder, though he moved away from the river.

Then the floor was gone and he tumbled into space. The smell of rotting flesh assailed him. A horrible, stinking ooze enveloped him. His hand touched a shape unmistakably a human skull. He'd fallen on a mound of decomposing corpses. A scream tore from his throat. His chest heaved. Sweat popped out on his forehead. He clawed at the tangle of bodies, pushed aside leg bones, ribs, skulls. Amidst the clatter came a metallic sound. His wife's urn, dented and scarred, the cold surface slimy to his touch. He wiped it on his jacket.

A whisper: *"Matt, get up."*

Emily.

His dead wife was calling to him. He clutched the urn, scrambled over bodies and bones and clambered out of the pit. Bile rose in his throat and he vomited, the convulsive expulsion splashing his boots.

He set down the urn, wiped his face and brushed away tears. The smell of putrid flesh clung to his clothes. A beam of light—like a motorcycle headlight—slit the darkness on a distant horizon, reflecting off a waterfall roaring over a cliff to his left, the precipice he had stumbled over. His throat was parched. The water drew him. He clambered to it, held his hands in the flow, scrubbed off the corpse scum, then scooped up handful after handful of cool, clean water, and drank.

He walked back toward the pit and picked up the urn. It felt cool in his hands. The cover was missing. A gust of wind, a back draft from the falls, hit him. His wife's ashes were sucked out of the urn and enveloped him, blinding him, burning his skin. His motorcycle leathers were coated with it. He pawed at his eyes, scrubbed his cheeks raw. A faint smell of Emily's perfume drifted around him.

"Emily?" Two images collided in his mind: his wife smiling softly as she twirled a lock of dark hair around her finger, and her features contorted with rage as she splashed his body with gasoline.

"*Follow me. It's your only chance.*"

"Chance for what?"

"*Survival.*"

Her voice held a tone of reasonableness.

"*You can't go back.*"

The pit lay in shadow behind him.

"*This way.*"

He ran toward the light, but it seemed to get no closer, on and on across an endless plane. His motorcycle boots kicked up little puffs off the powdery dirt. At sea level you could see six miles, he knew, to the horizon. He could run six miles; his daily training routine was ten. But now, with fear tightening his chest, he fought for breath. Still he ran. The light—Emily—was his only alternative to the eternal darkness around him. If Emily was still alive—or had somehow been brought back to life—he must find her and put things right. All the laws of nature agreed that was not possible, but still he ran. By some miracle, he had another chance. He called her name as he ran across an endless alkaline desert beneath an impenetrable blackness. He could not tell if he was above ground or in a cavern of unimaginable immensity.

Gradually, Matt became conscious of a force pulling at him, drawing him forward, faster and faster. He had felt this force before, a pervasive, visceral power drawing at his deep core, as the moon pulls the oceans of Earth. Maybe this was what Emily felt, right before she died.

He stopped, bent forward, hands on knees, panting for breath. The headlight, if that's what it was, seemed no closer. "Emily." His voice rose in a helpless wail, calling her name again and again. This was madness. His wife was dead. Her ashes clung to his body. Emily was gone.

He felt the force again and stumbled forward, pulled off balance. He fell to his knees and dug his fingers into the fissured earth. He would not go on; there was no point. He would lie down and die, alone in this strange, unnatural place. He had heard the doctors talking in low voices: "… not much left of this guy's mind." That was the only explanation for this horrible place. It existed only in his mind—or what was left of it. Not much left after all the pills they'd fed him. Death was the punishment he deserved. He toppled face down onto the dry, cracked surface. Wherever the force was trying to take him, it would have to drag his lifeless body. This would be the end of it.

"Matt?"

The voice again—a far-away, echoing sound. Unmistakably Emily. Even if it was only in his head, he wanted to believe she was somehow alive. He staggered to his feet. His shadow slanted away behind him, the beam of light held steady on the horizon. "I'm here," he said. He turned a full circle. Emptiness in all directions. "Where are you?"

"I'm with you," she said.

Matt said, "I … went crazy after you died."

"You're not crazy. And you're alive."

"I took your ashes, got on the bike and headed into the mountains."

"Why?" she asked.

"I was looking for the Raavacon center. Trying to find out what happened to you and your mother, to make some sense of—the time after. The coordinates were still on your GPS but there was nothing there. Just brush and rock. My mind snapped and I just started riding as fast as I could— let the bike take me."

"Oh, Matt."

But as he'd raced along the canyon rim, the bike had suddenly veered toward the cliff. "It was like the bike was trying to kill me—or something was. And I was willing to let it. I don't really know who, or what, pushed me over the cliff. Half of me wanted to live; the other half wanted to die."

A shadow crossed the shaft of light in front of him, a row of men walking, heads down, trudging off into the darkness. Emily's voice again: *"Go straight ahead toward the light."*

The men slogged along, ignoring the man in ash-covered motorcycle leathers running toward them. One of them lifted his head as Matt drew near. Matt recoiled, stumbling on the hard-packed ground. The man had no face. Where his eyes, nose and mouth should have been was a patch of pale skin.

Matt dodged the faceless man and ran again toward the light. Emily's voice: *"On your left there's a hill. Go that way."*

"It's pitch dark up that way."

"Please trust me, Matt. Go straight up the hill."

The ground rose quickly, soil becoming rocky and loose. Matt's feet slipped; he fell to his knees.

"Get up," Emily's voice urged, *"Hurry."*

He looked around him. Total darkness again. He pawed at the rocks, fingers scraping the crumbling surface. He kept climbing, crawling on hands and knees.

"You're almost to the top, keep going. Can you see anything behind you?"

"No. Just dark."

"Get up. Run."

He jumped to his feet, crested the hill and leaped forward into the darkness. He tumbled forward over the peak and fell down a steep rocky face. A faint red glow blossomed around him. In front of him a ravine stretched to infinity, right and left, between black stone walls. The floor of the ravine moved, something alive there—a mass of slithering creatures roughly the size of rat terriers. Their squirming, lizard-like bodies looked made of chrome, shimmering silver in the faint pink light of their glowing tongues. They swarmed across the rocks, chrome teeth snapping, the light brightening as more of them opened their mouths, exposing their neon tongues.

Matt recoiled in horror, trapped on a narrow ridge, feeling the force pull him toward the insane cluster of monsters. He took a tentative step toward the lizards. Many bared their teeth, rose on their hind legs, hissing and brandishing claws.

"Emily, what should I do? What can you see?"

"Scream at them, run as fast as you can. There's a tunnel a little ways ahead. They seem to be afraid to go in there."

No choice but to trust her. Matt screamed and jumped into the glittering mass.

One of the creatures, larger than the rest, slithered toward him. Matt kicked it with his knee-high boot. It squealed and toppled back into the reptilian mass. Its comrades set upon it and tore it apart. A red-black slurry spread across the rocks. The creatures were on him, teeth tearing at his boots, clinging to his leather pants legs. With a vicious backhand he knocked them away. Their cries echoed louder and the smell of meat and burnt metal rose around him. One of the creatures clamped its jaws on his bare hand. The razor teeth tore his flesh. He screamed in pain, ripped it loose and threw it at the rock wall, crushing its head. It slid down the rock leaving a slimy trail, a viscous mixture of blood and oil

More of the creatures leaped on their fallen comrade, leaving a gap ahead for Matt. He dashed forward, lost his footing on the slimy floor and fell face down on the rocks. He covered his head with his arms. Teeth pulled at the back of his leather jacket.

Dozens of the shiny creatures clung to his coat. He struggled to his feet tearing at their bodies with his hands. One worked its way inside his collar, going for his throat. He screamed, yanked its tail and pulled it free. It twisted toward him, snapping at his face. He threw it against the rocks.

"A ledge, straight ahead," Emily said. *"Jump."*

Matt leapt into the darkness. The ledge caught him at the waist and sent him tumbling forward. The glow from the chrome creatures' neon tongues revealed the opening of a cave. He crawled inside and fell on the rocks, panting for breath. The sound of rushing water came from somewhere far below him.

"You sent me straight into them, Emily."

"There was no other way," she said.

"You're punishing me."

"Helping you."

"If this is your idea of help, you can go to hell." A rueful chuckle. "Where I am already."

He climbed to his feet and fumbled his way down the tunnel, putting distance between himself and the metallic lizards.

They were a shimmering, squirming mass behind him. He still shook from the horror of their attack. Pain like fire ran up his hands and arms. Blood trickled from a bite on his neck.

The flickering light receded and he was again in total darkness, feeling his way to nowhere.

Chapter Two

Matt slumped onto the stone floor, exhausted. In the blackness of the cave, faint images swam into his mind. Black granite engraved with "Joyce Graves, Servant of Glory." Emily's mother. Emily's car in flames, crushed against the tomb.

On her last day on earth, their arguments had finally escalated into violence. Matt found her in his workshop pouring gasoline on his tools. "Emily, what the hell is the matter with you? You want to burn down the house?"

"You're screwing Cynthia Gilbert!"

"Emily, she …"

"Means nothing to you?" She splashed gas in his face and fumbled in her pocket for her lighter. He slapped her. She flipped the lighter to flame, pitched it at his head, and ran out to the carport. Her Nissan Sentra roared to life and squealed out of the driveway. Matt jumped on his Harley and went after her, barely escaping going up in flames with their house.

His phone rang. He tapped his earpiece. Emily screamed, her voice tinny in his ear. "Matt! I can't stop—"

Her car swerved into the cemetery, crashed through wrought iron gates. Her mother's black crypt loomed out of the snow. The car slammed into it head-on. Matt jumped off the bike, let it fall on the grass.

His wife's body was crushed behind the wheel of her car. Blood trickled from her mouth, painting her lips ghastly red, staining her white silk blouse. Matt ran to her, pushed her hair, thick with blood, out of her eyes. She stared at the sky, face a frozen mask. The light faded from her eyes. He tore aside the airbag, hugged her to him, called 911 on his cell phone. Emily was beyond comfort. Gradually, the warmth in her body faded.

He pulled her closer, whispering her name, begging her forgiveness. A moment before he had wanted her dead, now he prayed she would live. Sirens wailed. Three men in dark blue uniforms piled out of an ambulance and ran toward him.

They laid Emily's body on a stretcher and rolled her away. One of her pale arms slipped off the gurney and dangled. He tried to call to the paramedics; could summon no voice.

The third paramedic knelt beside Matt and pulled out a hypodermic needle. As he bent closer, his face metamorphosed into a shiny silver mask. He bared a row of needle-pointed teeth. Matt jerked his arm away and scrambled backwards. The man—the creature—was gone.

He spent a week in the hospital, heavily sedated. The doctors sent him home with bottles of pills. He stumbled through the next weeks, scarcely able to talk, certain he had lost his mind. The day Emily died, he had seen *something*—some malevolent creature he could not understand. But that creature hadn't killed Emily; her death was his fault. He had driven her to flee.

After Emily's service, his friends drove him to the crematorium, held his arms as he watched her remains disappear into the fiery chamber. They pulled him back when he tried to jump into the fire after her. In the weeks that followed, he gave himself over to the pills.

The memories were horribly vivid. He stared at his watch. Almost noon—or was it midnight? What did it matter? In the pale light of the dial he caught a glimpse of the sleeve of his jacket, still coated with Emily's ashes. The light faded and disappeared. The watch was dead, the blackness of the cave now total. Matt stumbled forward, arms outstretched before him.

❧

Emily watched Matt stumble along. Her mother's image appeared on the cavern wall in front of her.

"Let him suffer," Joyce said.

"He's panicked. We're torturing him," Emily said.

"That's the idea. Break him. Make him agree to anything you say. That's all that matters."

"He doesn't deserve this. Why can't we help him?"

"After what he did to you?"

"What about what I did to him?"

Joyce said, "Forget about all that. It was in another world."

"Mother, where are we, what's happening?"

"Never mind all that."

"I'm dead, Mother. There doesn't seem to be much point—"

Joyce jabbed a finger at her daughter. "You do as your Mother tells you."

"That's all I've ever done—but that was in another world."

Joyce said in that familiar, ice-cold voice, "Don't you ever sass me, child."

Her scowling image faded, but her words echoed over all the years of Emily's life.

An hour later—or was it two? Matt, gasping for breath, stopped walking. Blackness in every direction.

"Emily?"

Silence.

His ear caught the faint sound of rushing water and his thirst returned. Was it the sound of the river that had brought him down to this terrible place? Perhaps it would show him the way out. The idea of going down farther, following the course of the water, terrified him. Instinct told him to go up, get out of this hellish hole.

The feeling of being utterly alone was so strong that he began to break down, tears leaking from his eyes. Emily had tricked him, purposely led him to the horrible chamber of lizards that had nearly torn him apart. Led him to oblivion and then deserted him. He wept, deep sobs echoing in the darkness.

She had been justified, he supposed, but he hadn't planned to have an affair with Cynthia. He remembered being with her in the back seat of his Lexus. Cynthia reached between his legs, squeezed his genitals. Matt felt himself grow erect, unzipped his leather pants, his need for relief terrible. Cynthia moaned as his hand slid up her dress. He felt her wetness. A frenzy of lust overtook him.

Emily slipped into his fantasy now, black panties sliding down her hips, breasts thrust out. He touched himself, pulled his hand away, glanced around at the blackness. She might be up there watching. The urge faded.

Of course, Emily found out about the affair. They tried counseling but neither of them was ever fully present during the sessions. His wife became a cold, angry shadow of herself. Her mind was somewhere else. He couldn't bring himself to love her, even get close to her. She, of course, responded in kind. Finally, seeking vengeance, she set the house on fire and tried to kill him.

Why, then, was he so obsessed with her? If any guy had told Matt his wife tried to burn him alive, he would have advised the guy to run away and get a new identity.

But it hadn't been the real Emily, it hadn't. Something had happened to her up in that damn conference, something she couldn't talk about. It had changed her. Almost like Joyce had put some kind of spell on her. And he hadn't done anything about it, just felt sorry for himself and watched it happen. He'd failed her, and, to top it off, had cheated on her.

Now, her voice was his only link to the outside world. He shouted her name. His voice came back, a hollow echo, cathedral-like, but there was no church down here. He took a few steps forward. His forehead collided with the rock wall. He staggered back. Blood trickled down his forehead. He wiped it away and groped his way along the wall.

The rock felt smooth underfoot, like a path worn by long use. Maybe it was the men with no face. Matt pictured a vast cavern peopled with the faceless creatures. Since there was no light, no need for eyes. Or ears. Nothing to hear but the darkness. No one to talk to. No need of a mouth. No need of a mind. A thought chilled him: he, Matt Thanos, was on their path.

A faint scuffling sound ahead evolved into the sound of running footsteps. He flattened his back against the wall. The footsteps approached. A pink glow rose, and he saw another of the faceless creatures running toward him. Matt turned to see where the creature was running. The light came from a bend in the tunnel, echoing now with the hissing and clattering sounds of the lizards. The faceless man was running toward them.

"No, stop! Not that way!" Matt cried.

The creature slowed and turned to Matt, head tilted, like an animal hearing an unfamiliar sound. It waved its arms, pointing toward the blackness into which Matt had been heading. A frantic pantomime of fear: danger that way. What could be worse than the metallic reptiles toward which the faceless man was running?

Matt reached for him, but the man dodged away and ran on toward the ghastly pink light. The clattering sound grew louder. The faceless man, visible only in silhouette, leaped into the churning mass as Matt had done. His arms flailed, then he disappeared under their swarming bodies. The noise faded, the pink light dimmed.

Whatever horrors the faceless man had warned against, they could be no worse than the lizards. Matt felt his way along the wall, distancing himself from their feeding frenzy.

Chapter Three

Matt lay on the cold tunnel floor wiping sweat off his face, his mind swirling with the remnants of a feverish dream: Emily walking toward him, eyes aglow with love. Then her face morphed into a grinning metal mask filled with metal teeth. As he reached for her, she sank them into his arm. Pain like a burst of white light.

Now he lay in absolute darkness, hand throbbing with pain from the lizard bite. He had walked two or three hours along the monotonous stone corridor—no way to tell for sure, his watch unreadable in the darkness. His only goal had been to distance himself from the lizards and their flashing razor teeth.

On that long march he had tried to make sense of this strange new environment. The unreality of it all had knocked him off balance. Hearing his dead wife's voice was such a shock that he could think of little else. She had deserted him now, apparently. He let his mind drift back over the occurrences of his last few hours.

Every instinct, every sense focused on finding a way out of this place. He got up and started walking again, touching the wall for orientation. Think. Look at the sensory data as he had been trained. Focus on physical realities, the chrome lizards, the faceless men—creatures found no place on earth. Their existence told him nothing.

He walked on in total darkness; he had no idea how long. It felt like hours. His hands and arms had stopped bleeding but still hurt where the lizards had bitten and clawed him. His legs ached. He should be hungry. Perhaps the fear and dread that permeated his mind masked his bodily needs. Maybe he would, at some point, just collapse and die.

Or perhaps he was already dead. That was his biggest fear: that he was meant to suffer unending torment. Eventually, he too would become faceless, like those creatures that lived in eternal darkness at the bottom of the sea, evolving without eyes. The words froze him: "eternal darkness."

Every earthly vision of the afterlife contained this image, or lack of it. Surely his Greek ancestors had viewed the passage across the River Styx into the underworld as a journey to a world of eternal darkness. How he longed for light, any light. It was almost enough to make him backtrack to the lizard pit to bathe in the glow of their neon tongues.

The most horrifying thing he could envision was premature burial. Locked in darkness, fully aware of your fate. The Vestal Virgins of ancient Rome had been buried alive for the sin of infidelity, sealed in a crypt with a candle and a loaf of bread to prolong their torment.

He had heard stories of coffins being unearthed, their lids scored with fingernail scratches. Skeletons twisted, fingers broken from futile attempts to escape. The image of a grimacing skull filled his mind. He hugged himself, but could not stop trembling.

Then, as he walked, he was again aware of his body. Sweat ran down his cheeks. He unzipped his leather jacket, fanned himself as he walked. The floor felt warmer through the soles of his boots. A faint red light gradually revealed the cavern's form. It was perhaps twenty feet high, as wide as a two-lane highway. It seemed to be made of black rock, a lava tube forged by expanding gasses. The stark, hellish tube curved to the right a hundred yards ahead.

The tunnel opened onto a roiling pit of molten rock. The heat hit him and he scurried back. Trapped. Thirsty now, a thirst he had never known. The only moisture was the sweat running down his skin. He licked his dry lips. The heat seared his lungs. It was getting harder to breathe. He turned his back on the molten rock and retreated down the tunnel, fighting the urge to run.

Nowhere to run. Run for all eternity. Die like he had wanted to do a short while ago. Before he'd found Emily's spirit.

He thought again of the faceless man and his suicidal leap into the teeming mass of metallic reptiles. The man had been running from something even worse, had tried to warn Matt of this fiery cavern.

Logic demanded that the faceless man must have come from *somewhere.* He could not have come through that cauldron of molten rock. There must be another branch in this tunnel. Matt felt his way back the way he had come. If there was another passage, it had to be somewhere along this tunnel. No way to see it in this darkness. Despair and panic seized him.

Soon he would drop exhausted onto the rocky floor and die alone and invisible. And that would be the end of it. This was what death must be like. Black and silent. Maybe this was the true nature of hell. A void where there was nothing. Emily existed only in his consciousness. When he was gone, she would disappear forever—a thought he could not bear. He sat down on the floor, laid his arms across his knees, lowered his head and listened to the sound of his breath. Then the faintest of rushing sounds. Somewhere in the distance, through masses of stone, the river ran below him.

"Get up. You're almost there."

Emily's voice jolted him out of his despairing stupor. He forced himself to his feet, stumbled and steadied himself against the wall, looking for the source of the hollow, metallic echo. "Where are you?"

"Keep to the left side of the tunnel. Maybe fifty feet, there's a passageway."

"I thought you'd deserted me. My God, is there some way out of here?"

"This is the only way."

"The man with no face, he came that way?"

"I can't see everything."

He wanted to ask her what she *could* see. His only chance was to trust her, and he really didn't want to know. He shuffled forward in the darkness, hands outstretched, found the far wall, and crept along until finally his hands reached a space in the rock. The passageway. Cooler air flowed from it, streaming over his sweat-soaked face. He stood, eyes closed, breathing.

"This is the way out?" He hated the pitiful sound of his voice. Whining and begging, completely at her mercy. Was this her plan? Torture him, lead him endlessly through this torment?

"It leads up, that's all I can tell you."

The force had returned, pulling him forward. He stumbled into the opening, dropped to his knees, recovered and crept slowly forward. This tunnel was much narrower than the one he had been in. He could touch both walls, with his hands extended. The ceiling was unreachable.

A few feet in, his left hand met empty air. A branching tunnel. A sound of shuffling feet. Something moving toward him. He stopped.

"Keep going. Straight ahead."

"I feel that force pulling me again. What is it, what do you see?"

"Nothing."

Chapter Four

Matt felt his way along the narrow passageway past rows of voids in the rock face, each barely a foot wide, like narrow doorways. He heard things stirring. He had a sense that he was in a kind of dormitory. Creatures lived here. Maybe the faceless men. He imagined them shuffling around in tiny chambers, agitated by the stranger passing their doors. Their visitor was no less frightened. He imagined the faceless men creeping out behind him, following him in the darkness.

"Where am I going, Emily? Where are you leading me?"

"To the light."

It was true. Matt could make out dim contours of the tunnel walls, now. A speck of light in the distance grew larger until it became a quavering glow, fading in and out, gold to silver to green. He blinked, adjusting to the brightness. The path steepened. His legs ached with the effort of climbing. The air was cooler. Then he was out of the tunnel surrounded by iridescent sheets of color, dancing and oscillating, reminding him of the northern lights.

Overhead, an infinite black canopy pierced by sparkling points of light.

Stars.

Matt threw his head back. "Emily, I'm outside."

"You're not free yet."

"What do you mean?"

"You can't stay here. It's too cold."

Matt hugged himself. He zipped up his padded leather jacket. The light blazing around him offered no warmth. What a choice: go back into that hellish dark or freeze to death in the light. He turned and started back.

"Stop."

He stopped. "What is it?"

"You'll just have to trust me—hard as that might be."

Matt shivered. The ground under his feet had turned to ice. "What choice do I have?"

"Look up, find the North Star."

He found it easily. On many summer nights they had lain together on the lawn pointing at stars with their green laser pointer, naming the constellations. They had made love for the first time on a night like that, the grass cool under their bodies. The memory caught his breath. She had been frightened. He had asked her to trust him. It was his turn to trust her.

"Follow it."

Matt took a tentative step forward. The colored lights faded, revealing a long shining path made entirely of ice arching over empty space. "It won't hold me."

"Trust me."

Another step, and another. The ground fell away beneath him and he was walking along a narrow strip of ice arcing through space. The cold was all-pervasive. His teeth chattered and he beat his arms across his chest to keep warm. The bridge swayed slightly and he teetered on one foot. "This is no good. I'm going back."

"Keep going."

Matt edged forward. His dizziness increased. He got down on his knees. Ice water numbed his legs, but he pushed forward. In the distance the strip of ice disappeared into a greenish fog. A wind rose, pushing the strip into wilder and wilder arcs. Amazing that the ice ribbon held firm.

A faint rushing sound of water reached him as he crawled up the icy strand. He risked a peek over the edge. Far below, in a dark crevasse, a shiny ribbon of water raced along, surface churned to a white froth. It had to be the river that had pulled him into this horrible place. He had no illusions that he would survive a fall from this height.

Vertigo gripped him and he lay flat on his stomach, arms outstretched, fingers numb, body trembling. Freezing to death.

"Emily, how much farther?"

"I can't follow you any farther. I trust you to do the right thing—" Her voice cut off.

He felt the force again, the one that had propelled him off the cliff, pulled Emily's car into her mother's crypt, dragged him toward the lizards. He had no purchase on the ice, slid forward on his stomach, a human toboggan, until the ice beneath him became a blur.

The air darkened. Horrific faces swirled out of the fog. Monsters, with hundreds of empty eyes, mirrored faces contorted in silent screams. A phantasmagorical Halloween ride through hell.

The faces looked familiar, like the creature he had seen on the surface, but oddly modified. Tiny pearlescent white alligators, huge armadillos, hides glowing deep purple. Their mouths clicked open and shut, flashing yellowed teeth. Their cries and screeches deafened him. He closed his eyes and surrendered to the ice.

The ice strip arched downward until at last he was racing straight down, head first. The light around him faded from lavender to green to dark purple, like some animated minimalist painting. The grinning, snapping faces pushed closer now, rushing past his face in a continuous stream. He hurtled downward through the narrowing gauntlet—falling really—toward some unknown darkness. It grew warmer. The ice sheet he slid down melted slowly and he could feel water seeping into his motorcycle leathers.

His downward movement slowed. The light faded, the faces along with them, and he was again in total darkness, hovering in space. The only sound was the distant whisper of rushing water.

His grad school lecture notes came to mind: gravity is a force which causes any two bodies to be attracted to each other, with the force proportional to the product of their masses and inversely proportional to the square of the distance between them. But that meant somewhere there must be another gravitational mass pulling at him.

He had once believed that science could explain everything. If you had enough data the world was measurable, governed by laws and rules. But in this place, the familiar rules no longer applied. What good was science in a land where he slid down an ice bridge in a tunnel of slashing, screaming monsters with chrome teeth? He couldn't even rely on that one universal constant, gravity.

Everything started to unravel when Emily and her mother returned from the Raavacon conference, yammering about world-shifting energies abroad in the land. Good and Evil personified by the mythical beings, Raava and Vaatu. Incomprehensible gibberish, like the inscription on his mother-in-law's crypt, calling her a "Servant of glory." Matt had mocked their zealous chatter, until neither of them would talk to him.

Jocelyn Graves had called herself an 'enlightened occult practitioner.' It had been all Matt could do to keep a straight face. Her magic revolved around spells and spiders, snakes and sour mash bourbon. His mother-in-law, true to the cliché, had always hated him, accusing him of driving a wedge between her and her daughter, trying to make her look like a fool in her daughter's eyes.

She died mysteriously on a mountain in the Sierra Madres where she had gone soon after the conference—victim of a freak lightning storm, the sheriff told them. Her remains had been shipped back in a sealed lead box, which they had been advised not to open. The box was interred in the black marble crypt.

And now she was gone and he was trapped in this horrible place, and only Emily, apparently, could offer him any help. But now, she said she trusted *him* to "do the right thing"—whatever *that* meant.

He fought the urge to call her name. This had to be a tease of some kind. She seemed to have some kind of insight into what was going on, but she had shared little with him, except that she trusted him 'to do the right thing.'

He felt powerless to do anything. All trace of reality had disappeared on a wild slide down an ice bridge, over an enigmatic river, past a macabre kaleidoscope of horrific faces, only to end up again in silence and darkness. Matt seemed suspended in space, held between two opposing sources of gravity, caught in a contest between mystical forces.

As he floated weightless in the silent void, a stream of blue-green dots floated toward him, borne on invisible currents. He caught the odor of almonds. His science training kicked in. Cyanide. He drew in a frantic breath and held it. Emily had led him to his death. His rational mind fought back against his growing panic with a question. Why wait to kill him until now? She'd had so many opportunities.

He held his breath as long as he could, then drew a shallow breath. The almond scent was stronger now. He tried another breath, and then allowed himself to relax. No cyanide.

The spheres floated closer. He gauged their size to be something on the order of golf balls. They floated around him, slow-moving schools of bioluminescent creatures. Each one pulsed softly, as if breathing.

His ash-coated leathers showed blue-green in their soft light. A flash of movement drew his attention. One of the steel-toothed creatures that had flashed by him on the ice bridge now reappeared out of the darkness, snatched one of the creatures in its mouth and disappeared. The little floating creatures were edible, evidently.

He was suddenly aware of his hunger. A very positive sign. He was alive, the life force in him asserting itself. Even here in the blackness, the little round creatures held the promise of life—of survival. He caught one of them, cupped it in his hand. An animal? A plant? It had a velvety feel, the spines covering its body were soft, waving gently in his hand. He bit off a small cluster of spines. The creature did not react. He stuffed it in his mouth. It had a faintly salty taste, woody and earthlike, reminding him of mushrooms and sushi. He bit down and felt the creature move. How could he eat a still-living thing? The taste, however, spurred his appetite. He closed his eyes and chewed.

A soft, rubbery texture like some kind of sea creature—he found the taste pleasing. He swallowed a bit of the flesh, chewed and swallowed some more. The creature left a salty aftertaste, as he imagined a sea cucumber, or some other marine creature might. He reached for another one, devoured it in a similar manner.

He ate four in all. The ones still floating around him in the blackness showed no signs of alarm. In their collective glow, he could see some distance into the darkness to a rocky cliff face made of the same black lava he had traveled over before. Still he hung suspended in the air, felt a magnetic tingle in his limbs and, as his body absorbed the blue creatures, a sense of peace and well-being.

He floated ever so slowly, pulled by what he had come to think of as horizontal gravity, drifting past a featureless gray mountain. Glowing embers formed continuously around it, not falling on it but drawn to it in all directions.

They darkened and burned out, dropping onto the mountain.

He could no longer see the stars. He was passing back underground. Before, confinement had pushed him near panic, but now, he relaxed and closed his eyes, drifting peacefully amidst the bioluminescent creatures. They moved with him, drawn by the same force: horizontal gravity.

He stretched out his arms and legs, gliding through the darkness, eyes closed, with a smile on his face. His anxiety faded, his breathing deepened. The words, "bald head," came to his mind. He laughed out loud and the sound echoed off a wall he could not see. He was stoned. He ate several more of the bioluminescent creatures.

On their honeymoon, Emily and he, blind with love, had gone on a camping trip out in the Nevada desert. A group of campers in a VW bus offered to share some of their harvest. "Bald head" was a translation of the scientific term for *psilocybe cubensis*, better known as magic mushrooms.

Emily had seen strange creatures in the sky, spent the weekend chasing them, cackling madly. Matt had lain in his sleeping bag staring at the rock formations around him. Sandstone columns moved and twisted as if blown by the wind. The sun advanced and retreated, threw wild shadows, made him laugh out loud. The two of them had romped like puppies, lost in the wonder of each other, making love under the stars. They traveled the desert that summer, discovering each other, exalting in the natural world. Living in the moment. In love.

With that memory, peace enveloped him. He captured more of the floating blue spheres and filled his pockets. He closed his eyes and slipped into a breath-counting meditation, a habit he had picked up in his mushroom days. A soft, gold light grew around him, bringing a sense of peace. His torn hand had healed. He tented his fingers and bent his head. "Namaste." A second later he was asleep.

Chapter Five

"Do you have to smoke that god-awful stuff in here?"

"Relaxes you, Joyce. Give it a try." Matt handed his mother-in-law the pipe. She batted it away. Ashes flew across the sofa. Matt brushed at them, cursing under his breath. Emily chose that moment to come down the stairs carrying her suitcase.

She shook her head. "I wish you would grow up, Matthew. Leave the dope to the kids."

"Grow up? Look who's talking, the Stoner of Sedona. Remember that little desert romp on our honeymoon? You climbed in my sleeping bag …"

"Matthew, that's enough." She sat down the suitcase, bent to kiss him, hiding her smile from her mother. "I left you some information on the counter, in case you're interested in the retreat."

"Right." Matt picked up the pamphlet. Slick paper, four-color illustrations on every page—something out of a graphic novel. Lots of exclamation points. Raava was the spirit of peace and light; Vaatu, the spirit of darkness and chaos. Apparently, they planned to duke it out in the high desert that weekend. "For a mere $500.00 a pop you can witness, 'Raavacon,'" he said. How could anybody fall for this crap? "Why doesn't Vaatu have his own conference? Budget shortfall in hell this year?"

Joyce combed her fingers through her mud-brown hair and set her lips in a tight line. She and Emily wore matching denim skirts. "Make jokes if you want to." She slipped on a pink knit cap. "But you mock Vaatu at your peril."

Matt fought to keep a straight face. "Take notes for me."

Emily said, "Be nice. And don't—"

Matt held up his hand. "—forget to feed Baxter." At the sound of his name, their Jack Russell bounded into the room and squirmed onto Matt's lap.

"Maybe there's more to this world than your little science projects." Joyce crossed her arms over her bosom.

"I happen to believe that developing structural definitions for the planet is more than a 'little science project,'" Matt said. "I am not alone in that. The National Geophysical Institute has a budget of ninety-eight million dollars."

Joyce's scowl deepened. Matt held up his hands in defeat. No use fighting this battle again. He followed them out to the car and hugged Emily goodbye. They shared a long kiss, oblivious to Joyce's disapproval.

"You guys have a great week up there with Ragoo and Vato," Matt said, releasing Emily.

Joyce wagged an admonishing finger as she climbed into the car.

Matt poured dry food in Baxter's dish. The dog ignored the food, stood barking at the front door. "Hey, little guy, what's the matter?" Matt bent to pick the dog up, but the animal backed away growling.

The hair along his back stood up.

Chapter Six

Matt awoke on his back. The carpet of stars above him gave the desert a ghostly luminescence. He sat up. An endless expanse of sand and scrub brush lay before him. A row of blue hills broke the distant horizon. He was out of the labyrinth. He breathed deeply, soaking in his freedom.

A dog barked somewhere off to his right: a sharp yap. A familiar sound. Matt shook his head to clear away the fog in his brain. His old canine buddy had found him somehow. "Baxter?" The barking got louder. Matt smiled in spite of himself. "I love you. Shut the fuck up."

The barking came from the other side of a ridge about a hundred yards away. Matt called again and the dog appeared on the ridge top, his tail a blur. Matt jumped up and ran to him, scooped him up in his arms and scratched his ears. "Where did you go, boy?" Baxter had run away after Emily was killed. Matt gave up looking for him after a half-hearted search. The agony of loss and the ordeal of the funeral sent the dog to last priority. Somehow Baxter had found his way up here into the desert. The dog whined at him.

"She's gone, boy. Emily's gone. I'm sorry."

But her spirit still lived—somewhere back there under the ground, something he would have scoffed at a day ago. But he had heard her, smelled her perfume. Now she really was gone forever. Unless he could get back to her, and free her too, somehow.

The dog jumped from his arms, dashed back up the ridge, disappeared over the crest, then reappeared, barking, bouncing up and down in his exuberance. His body language cried, "Follow me."

Matt walked over the ridge and followed the dog along a narrow dirt track winding its way across the desert. The rock formations around him began to look familiar. He had ridden his bike somewhere into these hills looking for Raavacon, trying to understand what had changed Emily and her mother—what had possessed them. That, too, was more plausible after his experience underground.

The dirt track ended at a wooden barricade, painted with red and yellow stripes, mounted on a hinged pillar. A wooden shed the size of a phone booth stood beside it. Beyond the barricade was a scorched field of dust and gravel.

A man stepped out as Matt approached, tall, razor thin, face soft and pale, looking untouched by the desert sun. He wore an ill-fitting khaki uniform, pants several inches too short, shirt tight under his arms. His name tag, pinned crookedly on his shirt, read, "Tonto." He wore a sweat-stained cowboy hat with a gold security badge affixed to the brim. A holster bounced against his leg as he walked, scarcely able to contain the bone-handled .45 stuffed inside.

Matt pointed to the badge. "That your real name?"

"My mother named me 'Hector.' My dad thought 'Tonto' fit better."

"You know it means 'stupid' in Spanish?"

The watchman shrugged.

Baxter wagged his tail, put his paws on the man's knee. The watchman scratched his ears, smiled up at Matt. "Nice dog."

"Nice cowboy hat," Matt said.

"Fedora."

Matt gestured across the empty desert. "What are you guarding?"

"Raavacon. But the conference center moved—somewhere else."

"Where?"

"God, or somebody like him, only knows. You're covered with dust, must have traveled a far piece."

"It's not dust, it's ashes."

"Lord, *you're* the one. You been … down there. But you got out. Nobody's ever done that."

"What do you know about 'down there'?" Matt asked.

"I've heard …" Tonto looked down at his boots. "Nothin'. Don't want to know nothin'." A sly look crossed the watchman's face. "You didn't happen to pick up any cannon balls down there, did you?"

"Cannon balls?"

The watchman patted Baxter's head. "Stories is all I've heard. Glowy, floaty things. They supposed to make you really feel good."

Matt reached into his pocket, pulled out one the spiny blue spheres. It pulsed softly in his hand, glowed iridescent blue in the starlight. "This what you call a 'cannon ball'?" he asked.

"I'll trade you."

"For what?" Matt asked.

"Information."

"You said you didn't know anything."

Tonto shrugged.

"Fine." Matt handed him the glowing ball.

The watchman stuffed it in his mouth, chewed, smiled. "So what information—"

"Shouldn't be telling you this, but you're on some kind of list. Got a flyer tacked up in my booth. They want you bad. Here's my advice: stay away from the border, don't even get close. You won't like what's on the other side." The watchman looked over Matt's shoulder, eyes fearful.

Baxter growled. Matt spun around. Empty desert, dust devils teasing the sagebrush. "Who wants me?"

"My employers." Tonto scowled at himself. "I mean sort of. Not really. I mean you don't want to ask those kinds of questions around here."

"Just tell me what happened." Matt pointed to the broad blackened stretch of ground beyond the barricade where the conference center must once have stood. A solitary yucca plant, about eight feet tall, stood rooted in the gravel in front of the burned area. A hand-lettered sign near the plant read, "Do not feed the yucca!"

"Some woman broke the rules, that's all they told me."

"Who told you?"

"You don't want to know."

"So what happened?"

"Some kind of explosion. Nothing left but poor old Mr. Yucca there. I was off duty that day, lucky thing." Tonto lifted the barricade and strolled to the shrub. "Got any more cannon balls?"

Matt produced another, handed it over and pulled out one for himself. They chewed thoughtfully, regarding the solitary plant. Matt felt a pleasant buzz, but no sign of the golden light he had seen in the labyrinth. Apparently that came only from a deeper meditative state. "What do you feed a yucca?" he asked.

Tonto shrugged, accepted another cannon ball. Baxter sat in the gravel watching the exchange. The dog whined. "O.K. Here you go, boy." Matt tossed a cannon ball. It bounced off the dog's nose and rolled across the gravel.

"No!" Tonto screamed and scrambled after it. Baxter barked wildly. The yucca bent over and inhaled the blue orb into its spiny top. A flash of light blinded Matt, followed by a boom of thunder. The yucca exploded in a cloud of dust and sand. The blast lifted the two men and the dog off their feet, dumping them a dozen yards away. A gaping crater smoldered in the sand where the Yucca had stood.

The dog was the first one up, sprinting away over the hill, ears flat against his head. Matt called to him. "Come back, Baxter! It's okay!"

"No, it's not." Tonto stumbled to his feet, boots sliding in the gravel. His pistol dropped into the dirt. "Bad shit coming."

A line of black clouds formed over the crater. A sheet of rain marched toward them, across the sand, throwing up mud and mist. Matt snatched up the pistol and joined Tonto in a race up the hill.

They topped the hill and ran through the sagebrush on the other side. The sky behind them cleared and the starry desert sky again held sway. They stopped, gasping for breath. Baxter barked somewhere over the next hill.

"That way," Matt said. They set off again, at a fast walk this time.

Tonto looked over his shoulder at the now dry earth behind them. "That was damn close. That rain will *dissolve* you. That's how it happened at the … end. They say people just melted into the sand."

"Who says?"

"Don't ask me any more questions. I wasn't there." Tonto raised a defensive hand. "I won't have anything to do with that 'forbidden fruit' business."

Some terrible energy had been unleashed at Raavacon, something that still terrified Tonto. Emily and her mother must have been involved somehow. But what they had witnessed and how it had affected them was anybody's guess now. It might have been his bias, but Matt suspected that his mother-in-law was somehow involved in whatever destroyed Raavacon. Somebody hadn't followed the rules. As long as he had known Joyce, not following rules had been her credo. And the fallout had involved him, thrown him into a labyrinth as close to hell as he ever wanted to come.

This was his mother-in-law's doing. She had despised him from the start.

Baxter came running toward them trailing a thin could of dust, barking furiously.

"He's found something," Matt said.

Baxter trotted ahead, along a now faintly visible trail. The landscape had begun to look oddly familiar. Over a slight rise in the ground they could hear the sound of rushing water. There at the edge of the canyon wall, leaning against a Joshua tree, sat Matt's Harley, the bike that by rights should have been dashed to pieces and sucked into the underground river. Clearly, it was time to leave "reality" behind. Again.

Matt patted the gleaming black tank. "I thought I'd taken my last ride on this old Hog," he said.

"I know."

"You do? How is that possible?"

The watchman wore a thoughtful expression. "You have no idea what's possible out here."

Matt knew the bike would start, knew it was full of gas. Hell, maybe it didn't even need gas out here. He felt giddy. Life—and death—was full of possibilities. He threw a leg over the saddle. "Get on," he said.

The watchman shook his head. "You're crazy."

"Get on the damned bike."

Tonto climbed on, threw his arms around Matt's waist. Baxter climbed up and balanced on the seat in front of Matt. "Where are we going?" Tonto said.

"Which way is the border?"

"That way, but no … no."

Tonto's words were drowned in the Harley's thunder.

They were up to speed in a minute, sailing across the desert. Tonto's fedora flew off his head and drifted on the plume of dust marking their path across the trackless sand.

Chapter Seven

Dinner around the campfire consisted of their last four cannon balls. Baxter dozed on the sand.

Tonto warbled a few bars of Ry Cooder's "Across the Borderline."

Matt winced. "I don't think Willy needs any more backup singers. Know any Glen Campbell?"

"Horse you rode in on."

An odd camaraderie had grown between the two men, fueled in no small part by their steady diet of cannon balls. Tonto's fear had faded and he seemed unfazed to be traveling with a wanted man—wanted, at any rate, by his sort-of-not-really employers beyond the forbidden border. He no longer seemed threatened by Matt's presence. A complete change of attitude. There had to be a reason, and Matt wondered what it was.

Matt walked away from the campfire, unzipped his fly and stared up at the stars. He froze halfway through the act of relieving himself. There, outlined against the rising moon, was a solitary Joshua tree, its twisted silhouette reminding Matt of a tortured human form. The tree by the canyon rim where he had found the Harley. He had ridden the Harley hard across the desert for hours and gone exactly nowhere. He was living in world where the laws of physics had been repealed.

Tonto's fear of approaching the border had disappeared because he knew they were *never going to get there.* Matt pulled the watchman's pistol from his ash-covered jacket and marched back to the campfire.

Tonto was munching the last of his cannon balls, leaning back against a rock, feet stretched toward the fire. Matt jammed the pistol against the watchman's temple. "On your feet."

Tonto frowned, his body tense. "What's the problem?"

"You know what the problem is. We're in some kind of time warp here. We ride forever, we get nowhere. When were you going to let me in on the joke?"

"What are you talking about?"

Matt dragged the man to his feet. "I'll say this once. I'll get to the bottom of this and I'll get my wife back and none of your woo-woo deities are gonna stop me."

"Trying to save your life, man."

"I don't have a life. Not without Emily. She's … somewhere, and you're gonna help me find her."

"I'm just the watchman. But I have to admit I've been watching for you."

"What happens when I show up?"

"I'm supposed to report it."

"To who?"

"What does it matter? You figured out the time warp thing, and you weren't supposed to. That was to delay you."

"How long?"

Tonto shrugged. "Forever, if necessary.

"You came up with that little trick on your own?"

"There's trouble on the border."

"What kind of trouble?"

"Kind you want to stay clear of," Tonto said. "It's like when elephants fuck. All the little animals stay out of the way."

"I'm not staying out of the way. I'm going across. And you're gonna help me." He ground the barrel against Tonto's temple.

"I can bend the space-time continuum; you think I'm afraid of a gun?"

"I think you're afraid of your boss, whoever he is, finding out how much you let slip."

"How will he know?"

"I'll tell him." Matt shouted up at the star-filled sky. "Your boy here is breaking the rules."

"You have no idea who you're messing with here."

"Messing with you," Matt said. "Turn off the time warp thing. We're headed for the border." Matt stuck the pistol back in his jacket.

Tonto rubbed his temple. A trickle of blood ran down his cheek. "That hurt."

"For a guy who can control time, you've got a pretty thin skin."

"You think this is all a joke, but …"

"I've never been so serious. In fact that's been my problem all my life, never taking things seriously, making everything a joke. Emily always hated that part of me. But I am dead serious now." He grabbed the watchman's lapels. "You get me to the border or I swear I'll tear you apart."

"Ok, but no farther."

As they talked, Matt realized the force he felt in the labyrinth had returned and was pulling him forward, leaving the campsite and the Harley behind. He dragged Tonto back to the motorcycle. The watchman scooped the dog in his arms, climbed on and before Matt could reach for the starter, the Harley was flying across the desert under the bright burning stars.

❧

"See those lights over there?" Tonto pointed into the darkness. "Way station. Better stop there and rest. We're in real time now, and my ass is aching. This is the last stop before the border."

"Motel? Middle of nowhere?" Matt asked.

"Roadhouse. Rough place, but we don't have much choice. Just watch yourself."

❧

An angled edifice of weathered boards, crafted in the shape of a woman's head, rose out of the desert. Where the nose might have been hung a crudely-lettered sign: *White Knuckle Roadhouse.* Beneath the sign, the door—life-size glass lips—leaked faint yellow light. They slid open in an obscene smile as Matt and Tonto approached. A thin man in a fedora and leather vest leaned on the porch rail. "Nice ride." His lip curled in what might have been a smile.

"Fat Boy Special," Matt said.

The man spit into the street. "That *is* special."

Matt stepped onto the porch and returned the might-be smile. "It's a classic, friend."

Tonto nudged Matt forward. "Keep walking."

The glass door slid shut silently behind them and they stood in what could have been a movie set from an old western: Men sat drinking and playing cards at rickety tables. A guy in a derby hat and suspenders teased a waltz out of an ancient upright piano. A long mahogany bar ran the length of the room, a curving wooden stairway led up to a second floor. A woman in a green satin skirt posed on the top step, face hidden in shadows. All ignored the arrival of the two travelers.

It took Matt a second to realize what was odd: the floor was transparent, revealing a field of stars scattered on a backdrop of black. Matt took a tentative step out onto the glass, tapped it with his boot heel. Solid. He stepped toward the bar.

The bartender wore a red satin shirt, fabric taut across his belly. His silver belt buckle proclaimed him *Grand Champion calf roper*. A gap-toothed smile took the edge off his admonition: "Sorry, just closing."

"We need food and a bed for the night." Matt brushed ashes off his sweat-stained leather jacket.

"Little trail dust?" The bartender wiped the bar with a tattered rag.

"Ashes."

The piano player froze. The patrons set down their glasses, dropped their cards and slid back in their chairs.

"Holy shit. You're the guy," the bartender said. He reached under the bar. Baxter, still cradled in the watchman's arm, laid back his ears and growled. Someone at a back table snickered. "Watch it, Elmo. Looks like a mean son-of-a-bitch." Laughter.

The bartender laid his hands flat on the bar. "Best thing you can do is turn right around and—"

"A little food and a place to rest," Matt said. "We've come a long ways."

"Oh, I bet you have."

Tonto put the still-growling Baxter on the floor. The dog slipped on the glass, feet scrabbling for purchase. More laughter.

"Let's get out of here," Tonto said.

The woman in the green dress had disappeared.

The hostility in the air gave Matt new sense of purpose. Let them try to stop him. The way back with Emily lay somewhere beyond the border. Anyway, there was nothing left to be afraid of in this upside down world. He was probably already dead.

He stepped to the bar. "Beer."

"Maybe you didn't hear me …" Elmo, the bartender, said.

"Beer."

"One beer and then you're out of here, understand?"

"Got it," Tonto said.

The bartender popped a long-necked Ninkasi and slid it across the bar.

Matt tipped it back, drained it. "What do you mean, 'I'm the guy'?"

"All I'm gonna say. You had your beer, now get out of here."

Tonto scooped up the struggling dog and backed toward the doors. They slid open behind him and the skinny Harley critic from outside stepped through. "Better listen to the man," he said. "Can't have you boys here. It ain't safe. And you," he jabbed a finger at Tonto, "You had *one* job. Can't believe they made you the watchman, you little shit."

"What job?" Matt asked

"Callin' me a little shit?" Tonto put down the dog, produced a folding knife, and flicked it open with a thumb.

Harley boy sneered. "You haven't calculated the odds very good, have you little watchman?"

All the patrons stood up, pushed their chairs back and advanced toward the bar. Matt watched them in the mirror. A big man in a black leather coat led the pack. When they were a few steps away Matt smashed his beer bottle on the bar and spun around. "Nice cowboy hat," he said.

"Fedora." The big man swung a fist. Matt stepped aside and slashed the man's face with his bottle. Leather coat tripped and sprawled across the glass floor. He jumped back to his feet, grabbed a bottle off a nearby table and swung it at Matt's head. Matt raised his arm to deflect the blow. Glass shattered and the whisky sprayed his face, blinding him. The big man grabbed him in a bear hug. Matt head-butted him and the big man sank to the floor unconscious.

Baxter howled and launched himself at the cowboy by the door. The man took a step back, slipped on the glass and fell on his back. Baxter closed in, clamped his teeth on the man's crotch.

The bartender produced a fence rail wrapped with barbed wire from beneath the bar. He swung at Matt's head. Matt dodged and threw a fist at another of the cowboys circling him. The man fell, blood spraying from a shattered jaw. The floor ran with blood now, and the men around Matt began to slip and slide, hands pawing ineffectually at him. He jumped onto the bar and lashed out with his boots. Two more men went down. But the bar was slick with booze and blood, and Matt fell heavily on his back. The cowboys closed in.

Tonto jumped onto the bar beside Matt, brandishing his knife. He slashed a man across the chest, slicing through his leather vest and pearl button shirt and sending more blood splattering. The attackers stumbled back on a floor slippery as an ice rink.

A chair flew across the room, bounced off Matt's shoulder and crashed into the backbar mirror. A million glittering shards exploded onto the bar. Behind the mirror's frame stretched an infinity of stars, the same vista visible beneath the glass floor.

In the center of the frame a single bottle, filled with shimmering blue liquid, hung suspended in space.

The two travelers had forgotten the bartender. He leaped forward and slammed his fence rail across Tonto's forehead. The watchman toppled backward, head banging the dry sink behind the bar.

The attackers were regrouping. Matt raised his fists. A sudden movement in the shadows at the top of the stairs caught his eye. The woman in the green dress held a double-barreled shotgun. The barrel wavered in her grip.

Belatedly, Matt remembered the .45 he had appropriated from the watchman. He fumbled in his jacket. A tongue of fire burst from the shotgun. Shelves of bottles on the back bar blossomed into a fountain of booze.

Matt yanked out the pistol and raised it toward the stairs. The woman dropped the shotgun and disappeared down the hall. Something about the way her dark hair swung around her shoulders.

No, it couldn't be.

He leaped off the bar and slip-slid across the floor, holding the cowboys at bay with the pistol. "Emily, wait!" He took the stairs three at a time, then crept down the hall, pistol held out before him. A door stood open at the end of the hall, a pale blue light reflecting off the opposite wall.

Matt stepped into the doorway, pistol ready. Before him stretched a phantasmagorical cityscape: crystalline geometric forms stretched to the horizon, disappeared up into the stars. This, he guessed, was the border.

Emily was here somewhere. Though he hadn't seen her face clearly, it had to be her, again trying to kill him. He had to find her, make up for his transgressions. In spite of her trying to burn him alive and lure him to his doom in this strange afterlife—how much he'd hated her for it—he had to put his hate behind him. Let love grow again. But first he had to unravel the bizarre mysteries that surrounded him.

The stairs creaked behind him. Matt spun on his heel. Elmo, the bartender, red satin shirt torn and bloody, stumbled up the stairs. His eyes widened as Matt raised his pistol.

"The woman in the green dress, who was she?" Matt centered the pistol on the Elmo's chest.

"Never saw no woman in a green dress."

Matt cocked the gun. "Now would be a bad time to lie."

"Truth. Swear to Raava."

"That woman tried to kill me."

"Wasn't no woman," Elmo said.

"I saw her."

The bartender's expression changed, as if he recognized something about Matt he hadn't before. "Sometimes, you want to see something bad enough, you see it," the man said in a commiserating tone.

"It was Emily," Matt said. But maybe the man was right.

"Your woman?"

"Thought she was."

Elmo shook his head. "Lost your lady. Those stories tear the heart right out of me. I lost mine a few months back. Name was Tanya. The gods came and took her away. Never got over it."

"She died?" Matt lowered his gun a little. "Sorry to hear it."

"Worse. The gods *took* her—across the border. I can't think about what she's doing now—forced to do." He stared at the floor, remembering.

"You're helping us now?" Matt asked. "Turning traitor on your bosses? That's quick. A second ago you were trying to kill us."

"Heat of the moment. When you're scared all the time, sometimes your reflexes get the better of you. Let's just say this is for Tanya." Elmo inclined his head back down toward the bar. "Sorry about clocking your buddy. He's okay. I'll fix you guys some grub, find a bone for the dog."

Matt hesitated a moment, then pocketed his gun. He let Elmo take the lead and followed him back downstairs. "What's with the wanted poster?" he asked.

"The gods are angry with you, but I got no dog in that fight." Elmo held up his hands in a gesture of dismissal.

"The Gods are angry? Why?"

"You got out of the labyrinth," Elmo said. "Nobody's ever done that before, not without help. That sets a bad precedent."

"If this is not the labyrinth, where the hell am I?"

"No-man's-land, between the labyrinth and the border. You can think of us as border security. Though they haven't needed us much. Nobody's ever made it through."

"If I wanted to cross the border, how would I go about it?" Matt asked.

"I should never tell you this, but there might be a way."

Matt joined Elmo at the bottom of the stairs. The two surveyed the wreckage of the bar. "Buy you a drink?" Matt offered.

"I own the place, but thanks," Elmo said.

"It's the principle."

"Indeed it is."

They stepped over several comatose cowboys. Elmo fetched a bottle of Scotch. They clicked glasses. Matt said, "You guys are completely different from the poor souls down in the labyrinth. How did you happen to end up here?"

Elmo took a sip of scotch. "Damned if I know."

Tonto dozed, stretched out on the floor, face pale in the starlight filtering up through the glass. Baxter lay underneath a stool, working on his bone. As the Scotch got lower the bar faded around the three, leaving only empty sand and the stars beyond. After a while, Elmo told Matt what he knew.

Chapter Eight

Matt spat out a mouthful of sand and raised himself on his elbows. Baxter sat at his feet, gnawing a bone. Tonto lay face-down beside him, eyes closed. The White Knuckle Roadhouse had disappeared.

Tonto opened his eyes, rubbed the knot on his head.

"What happened to the roadhouse?" Matt asked.

"This close to the border, things float in and out. Like that over there."

Matt followed Tonto's pointing finger. A few yards away a rusty barbed wire fence stretched across the desert, fading into the distance right and left.

"That's the border," Tonto said. "Far as I go."

"I saw the border. That's not it."

"How do you know?"

"I found out some things while you were sawing logs in the bar. There's a whole city across the border, a whole country—a whole world for all I know. The way the bartender described it, it's more like the Greek idea of Mount Olympus. He said I should be looking for a different kind of mountain, where everybody's ashes end up."

"Why would you want to go there?"

"My wife—her spirit—might be there somewhere. I have to find her."

Tonto frowned. "What are you going to do then?"

"I don't know."

"How do you know she wants to be found?"

Matt didn't answer immediately. Building a life with Emily had given him a purpose he'd lacked. The first ten years of their marriage had been wonderful, full of laughter. They'd shared everything, even told each other their dreams. Her mother changed all that. Joyce's obsession with metaphysics and new-age religion rubbed off on her daughter. The two women withdrew into a world of their own, chanting, burning candles, sharing strange occult beliefs. Matt could not hide his contempt. It became a tug-of-war for Emily's attention between him and Joyce, and he lost.

He ended up sleeping on the sun porch with Baxter.

"I need to know what happened to her. I thought she was gone forever, killed in a car crash. But I heard her voice in the labyrinth. She guided me out." He looked at Tonto. "Elmo told me that's never happened before."

"Never has," Tonto said. "Something about her ashes going down into the labyrinth threw off the balance of things. They can't have people getting out of that place."

"Who's this 'they' you keep talking about?"

"They control everything. You do or say anything against them and … you saw that acid rain storm. I don't want to be dissolved into the sand. You learn to goddamn follow orders out here."

"As far as I can see, I've got nothing to lose."

"Don't be so sure. Remember what happened to you down in the labyrinth."

"What do you know about that place?"

"Well, nothing really. I've just heard—"

"You heard. That's just it. You take everything on faith."

Tonto shrugged. "Faith is all we have."

Matt stood up. "But what if none of it's true, what if there are no angry gods over there across the border, just some bullshit they tell you to keep you in line?"

"Some of their 'bullshit' put you down in the pit."

"And I got out. We're about to test my theory." Matt walked to the fence, pulled down the top wire and stepped over. "You coming?"

Tonto looked around and shrugged. "I guess I'm fucked either way."

Matt pointed his finger at Baxter. "Sit. Stay." The dog whimpered and sat down on the sand.

They walked together across the sand. Matt remembered what Elmo had told him. The powers that be derived their power from emotions. The calmer you kept your mind, the less visible you became, the less attention you attracted. He had to approach the border in a calm state of mind.

❧

The desert was bathed in an eerie twilight. Before them rose a wall of glass and crystal. That world existed at 90 degrees to the desert where he stood. Mirrors on the crystal walls threw rectangles of hard, blue-white light onto the sand around Matt. People in white robes and sandals walked, trance-like, down transparent streets on what would have been walls in the world Matt knew.

Matt sat down cross-legged on the sand. Tonto, not understanding, sat next to him.

"Clear your mind," Matt told him. He explained what he'd learned from Elmo. "Strong emotions fuel the gods here. We want to stay under their radar."

"How do we do that?"

"Close your eyes and focus on your breathing. Count from one to ten, over and over until you see a gold light around you."

Tonto closed his eyes. "You sure?"

"Relax, try it."

Matt followed his own instructions, felt himself calming down. Gold light grew around him. He opened his eyes. Tonto sat beside him, eyes closed. "You see the gold light?" Matt said.

"Beautiful."

"Open your eyes."

A line of ground fog swirled at the base of the glass wall. The two travelers stood up and walked toward the mist. A row of white-robed guards stood shoulder to shoulder before them

Acting on instinct, Matt stepped into the mist. The guards ignored them as they approached. "They can't see us," Tonto whispered.

Just beyond the wall was a wide glass corridor. On the left, the desert landscape with its endless border fence appeared as a great wall of sand reaching from the transparent plane where Matt stood to a star-filled sky above. Baxter ran back and forth on the sand, barking.

The change of perspective was dizzying. Matt drew a breath, willed himself to relax. Tonto stumbled out of the fog bank behind him and looked around wide-eyed. "Where is everybody?" His voice was a hoarse whisper.

"At the Game," Matt said.

"What game?"

"According to Elmo, the gods send teams to challenge each other. Everybody goes to watch, mandatory."

"What team are we on?"

"I don't think we were invited. They don't know we're here. I hope."

They hiked for half an hour through an Escher-like landscape where up and down were forward and back, and the structures around them were a trackless jumble of geometric shapes built of a mixture of mirrors and translucent blue-white panels. It reminded Matt of watching astronauts drifting in space, floating in the absence of gravity. "Horizon" was a meaningless term. There was no up or down, though some force held them to the glass landscape. Matt realized this place must be the source of horizontal gravity, a hidden world with a mass rivaling that of Earth's.

A flurry of movement in the distance caught Matt's eye, shapes swirling through space, a cloud of bodies whirling in unison, like swallows looking for a nest, above some kind of arena. This must be the place Elmo had described.

The Game was on.

As they got closer, Matt made out individual figures drifting around each other: a mixture of faceless club-wielding fighters wearing tufted helmets and leather breast plates, and pale blond men dressed only in loose white robes. The robed combatants, though empty handed, seemed quicker and more agile than their leather-belted adversaries, easily dodging their clubs, sometimes even snatching them away.

Bleachers rose on either side of the arena, packed with spectators. Men and women, all wearing belted white robes and crowns of laurel leaves, stared at the combatants in slack-jawed fascination.

How could the faceless men see to defend themselves? The battle was a swirl of bodies, three-dimensional football with a hundred on a side. They played the game, if that's what it was, in total silence.

"Reminds me of the Greeks," Matt whispered.

"Or Romans. How long does this game go on?"

"According to Elmo, until one side is destroyed." Matt searched the rows of faces.

"What are you looking for?"

"Tanya, Elmo's girlfriend." He explained how the gods had taken her and turned her into a sex slave, and that Elmo had told him how to cross the border on the condition that Matt rescue his lady.

A moan rose from the crowd. The tide had turned. One after another, white-robed fighters went limp and drifted down toward the bleachers like snowflakes until, finally, the sky was empty of white-robed warriors. The faceless leather-belted fighters drifted into a loose formation, raising and lowering their clubs in a victory dance.

Matt continued scanning the crowd. He noticed a woman looking at him. She took off her head scarf, revealing the only black hair in a sea of blonde. "Down there." He pointed. "Third row. Raven black hair, like Elmo said."

The woman kept her eyes on them, ignoring the victorious warriors in the air above her.

"Has to be Tanya." He headed around the upper perimeter of the arena, in her direction. The spectators started leaving their seats.

"They're just gonna let us take her?"

"Who, the gods? Where are they?"

"I don't think they have to be here to watch the game. Gods see everything." Tonto glanced over his shoulder.

"They haven't seen us."

"Maybe. Not yet."

Matt and Tonto pushed their way through the departing crowd, collecting scowls and elbows for their trouble. Up close, the white-robed figures bore an eerily similar appearance: bland, even features, uniformly blonde and blue-eyed.

"These are scary fucking people," Tonto said.

The crowd began to thin. Robed figures filed past, cursing, arguing with each other about the Game. Matt and Tonto fought past another exit. Matt noticed that, as people left the arena, their frowns of disappointment morphed into beatific smiles. Emotional responses. This was how the gods kept the population under control. Matt forced himself to relax and remain neutral.

Stay below the emotional radar.

The black-haired woman trailed the departing crowd. There was a sensuality in her movements that distinguished her from the others. Matt couldn't help noticing the roll of her hips as she climbed toward them up the glass stairway. Elmo said she had the face of an angel. He wasn't wrong.

She shot nervous glances around her, pulled her robe tighter as Matt and Tonto approached.

"Tanya?"

She nodded, her eyes downcast, mouth set in a tight line. "You're not supposed to be here."

"Your boyfriend says he still loves you."

"How can he, after what I've become?" She hid her face in her hands. "Is he all right?"

"He's fine. He knows you're not here of your own free will. We can take you out of this place if you help us."

She looked up, sadness in her eyes. "Nobody gets out of this place."

"Nobody ever got out of the labyrinth either," Matt said.

She laid her hand against her breast, mouth open in surprise. "You're the one—the Ash Man. How did you get in here? There's a row of guards all along the wall."

"There's a way past them."

As the crowd drifted away into the maze of glass and mirrors, the walls surrounding the arena darkened, leaving them standing in dim gray light.

"This is what they call a 'privacy fog,'" Tanya said. "The higher your rank, the thicker 'fog' you get. I'm the lowest rank—a concubine." A bitter laugh.

"Will you help us?" Matt asked.

"You're asking me to risk my life," she said.

"All our lives," Tonto said

"I'm asking you to take a chance on having a life."

Tanya studied Matt's eyes. She gestured for him and Tonto to follow her, and led them down into the arena. "Sit down here beside me. No one comes here after the Game is over." They all sat cross-legged in the middle of the glass field. The privacy fog had thickened.

In the darkness, Matt concentrated on the sound of her voice, throaty, melodic. An erotic timbre.

"He forces me to have sex with him." she said.

"He?"

"Raava."

"I thought he's supposed to be the spirit of peace and light. My mother-in-law talked about him all the time."

"He stands in front of me every day in human form. Naked."

"And he forces you … ?"

"Oh, yes."

The image of Tanya in a sweaty tangle with a god was too much for Matt. He hurried to fill the silence. "Tonto here, the watchman at Raavacon, told me there was trouble over here across the border. Something about 'forbidden fruit'?"

"There's some fancy Greek name for them but most people call them cannon balls." Tanya said. "You use them to keep your emotional level below what the gods need to control you, that's why they're forbidden. The gods can't tolerate not being in control."

Matt nodded. "That's what Elmo told me."

Tanya sighed. "Elmo always likes to know everything about everything. Mostly what cannonballs do is make you drunk."

"They can do a lot more than that." Matt explained he and Tonto had done breath-counting meditation outside the glass wall.

"I thought it was crap at first," Tonto said, "but we walked right through that row of guards. We were invisible."

Matt pulled a cannonball from his pocket. "This is your ticket out of here. Swallow it and just keep counting your breaths, one to ten, over and over. You'll see a gold light. Then you're invisible."

Tanya's disbelief was plain on her face. "Never heard of anything like that. The gods have so much power …" She shuddered. "They gain it from human souls. They pull you in and drain off your energy—like a battery. That's what Raava and Vaatu fight about. Whoever gains the most souls has the most power. It's been that way for millennia."

"God and the Devil," Matt said. "That myth's in every religion."

"Only this is not a myth. I'm living in the middle of it. The energy from all those souls is stored in a place called the Mountain of Ashes. They trap your soul there forever while they bleed off your spiritual energy, drain you to oblivion. True believers want to get onto the mountain. They welcome control. It brings comfort. Every form of refuge has its price."

"The Mountain of Ashes," Matt said. "I've seen it." He remembered the gray incline he had drifted past, how it had risen to block out the stars. How glowing embers formed around it. Now he realized what they were: human souls drawn through the veil to Raava and Vaatu's dump site for the dead.

Tonto knelt on the glass. "Dangerous territory, my friend."

The distant rumble could have been thunder, but the sky above the arena grew brighter. The privacy field dissipated, exposing them to the hard, crystal glow of stars. A glass boulevard lined by rows of mirrors appeared, descending into the arena. The thunder reached a crescendo, and a male figure materialized in the boulevard, stern and bearded, dressed in blue robes tied with green satin cords, his image reflected to infinity left and right.

Raava.

He raised his arms and the thunder stopped. His arms and shoulders were heavily muscled. A flowing white pompadour framed a face ravaged with age. He smiled at Tanya. She pasted a seductive smile on her face, and whispered to Matt and Tonto out of the corner of her mouth, "Go back to the border. I'll keep him occupied."

"We'll wait for you," Matt whispered back,

Tanya danced over to Raava, vixen-like, trailed a finger across his chest.

"Get ready to run," Matt said.

But the god ignored them, focusing on the black-haired woman. She untied her sash. Raava opened his robe. She knelt before him.

"Close your eyes, deep breaths," Matt said. "No emotions."

Guttural moans echoed in the arena. The slap of flesh on flesh. Matt opened his eyes. Tanya and Raava lay intertwined, slippery with sweat, on the glass floor.

⸱

A group of the white-robed denizens, men and women, clustered around Matt and Tonto as they hurried back toward the border, blocking their path.

"What is your purpose here?" a man demanded

"We're just leaving," Matt said.

"We're peaceful," Tonto added.

"Yes, but that was not the question. You crossed the border. No one does that in peace."

"Who told you that?" Matt asked.

"Our god," a woman said. "He tells us everything." The others nodded. "He has given us a kingdom of eternal peace. Nothing must intrude on that." The group crowded closer, smiling as they raised their fists.

"Did he tell you how he takes women and turns them into sex slaves? Did he tell you how he runs this kingdom of peace and light on the energy of dead souls?"

"A lie. Blasphemy. You are servants of Vaatu." The crowd had become a mob. Matt and Tonto pushed their way through, dodging blows. They ducked into an alley, found it blocked by a wall of mirrors. Tonto slipped on the glass and fell. A dozen people crowded around, punching and slapping him. Matt waded in, grabbed him and pulled him to his feet. They stood back-to-back, facing the crowd.

"C'mon, you pussies," Tonto whispered. He stomped one man's bare foot and the man fell screaming to the glass.

The crowd backed away. Matt and Tonto pushed their way through the crowd and ran. The white-robed pack pursued them for a distance, but then seemed to lose interest, apparently content to return to their world of peace and love. They faded into the distance.

"Beat up by hippies," Tonto said. "Hell of a thing."

"We need to calm ourselves," Matt said, slowing to a walk.

Tonto matched his stride. "We owe Tanya one."

✦

The fog bank at the border settled around them, obscuring the division between the glass and the endless desert sand. Matt's little white dog sat, barely visible, on the vertical wall of sand. He jumped up and started barking as Matt and Tonto approached.

"Let's go," Tonto said.

"No. We wait for Tanya. We promised her."

"*You* promised."

"You said we owe her."

Tonto threw his head back in frustration. "If they find us, we're finished."

"We wait. Relax. Close your eyes."

"Ash Man, where are you?" Tanya's voice came through, faint and muffled by the fog.

"Tanya," Matt whispered. "Over here." She ran to him.

The fog parted. Raava stalked toward them, naked body still slick with sweat.

Tanya whispered, "He's filled me with his god fluids. His life force is depleted. This is the only time he's vulnerable."

"So, we have a traitor," Raava said. Depleted or not, his voice was thunderous, belying his human dimensions. He grabbed Tanya's shoulder. She fought to keep her expression neutral—show no emotion.

Matt pulled her free of Raava's grasp, tucked her behind him and turned to do battle with the god. Raava batted him away with a backhand blow, grabbed Tonto and held him up by the neck. "My loyal watchman? Two traitors."

Matt lay dazed on the glass boulevard. This was the end. How could he fight against a god? Still, he had to try. He struggled to his feet. "Put him down," he shouted. Raava obliged by throwing Tonto to the ground with a force that knocked him unconscious. A trickle of blood ran from the corner of Tonto's mouth.

Raava spread his arms and said in his booming stentorian voice, "All traitors die."

"Not today." Matt bent and charged, plowing his head into Raava's unprotected stomach. The god woofed out a puff of air and sat down hard on the glass boulevard, legs splayed. A group of his white-robed subjects strolled by on a glass panel overhead. One woman snickered and the group hurried off.

Raava stood up, casting Matt aside with another back-handed blow, and roared. The glass ceiling crashed into pieces around him.

Matt landed on his back and a sharp jolt of pain went up his spine. But he struggled to his feet again, and crouched to face the god. "My wife, Emily, where is she?"

Raava approached Matt more warily this time.

"She's where *you* put her," Raava said.

"*You* dragged her into the labyrinth."

Raava shook his head in disdain. "You can thank my black-hearted enemy, Vaatu, for that."

"I want her back."

Raava pointed his finger. "You make no demands of me. I can destroy you in an instant."

"You've destroyed yourself," Matt said. "Your kingdom of peace is a sick, twisted joke. Control your subjects' emotions, power your empire with the souls of the dead. I know about your Mountain of Ashes."

Raava's face contorted with rage. Blue sparks danced from his fingertips.

Out of the corner of his eye, Matt saw a flash of red satin through the fog shrouding the border, the gleam of a silver belt buckle. Elmo, the bartender from the White Knuckle Roadhouse, stepped out and handed Matt a bottle of shimmering blue liquid. "Drink this."

"What—?"

"Cannon Ball Cordial."

Matt stared at the bottle a beat, pulled the cork and tipped it back. The taste was somewhere between mouthwash and a cheap Chardonnay but the effect was immediate. A feeling of warmth and well-being flooded his body. Gold light grew around him. He felt loose, fearless, and capable of anything. "And I know something else," he said to Raava, holding up the bottle defiantly. "There's a way to beat you."

Raava looked around, puzzled.

Matt realized he was invisible to the god. "You're contemptible," Matt said. "You tear wives away from their husbands, keep them as sex slaves. Screw them in the amphitheater."

A shout burst from the fog: "You son-of-a-bitch. She's mine!" Elmo crouched in an awkward martial arts stance. He waved at Tanya. "I'm here, babe." He threw himself at Raava, screaming curses, throwing wild punches. Raava grabbed his neck and squeezed. Elmo's body convulsed, outlined in sparks, then collapsed, body deflated like a balloon.

Tanya knelt beside his flattened remains. "You crazy damned fool," she whispered.

Raava reached for her. She slid away and disappeared into the fog, pulled as if by an unseen force. A few moments later, Tonto's body slid across the glass into the fog, seemingly of its own volition. Raava looked up and down the empty glass boulevard. "Where are you, Ash Man?"

"I've found your forbidden fruit, asshole," Matt's voice echoed through the fog.

Chapter Nine

After they had slipped across the border, Matt and Tanya, each holding an arm, dragged Tonto toward the barbed wire fence. His boots left twin trails in the sand. He opened his eyes and grimaced in pain. They laid him down and Tanya knelt to wipe blood from his forehead. Baxter ran toward them. Matt bent to scratch the dog's head. "Good dog, you waited for me."

Baxter growled, laid his ears back.

"What is it?"

Thunder crashed and a black cloud appeared under the stars. A line of torrential rain moved toward them. A family of prairie dogs ran before the deluge. The water caught them and they dissolved into the sand. Tonto struggled to his feet. "Run for it," he said. "Don't worry about me." He took a few faltering steps toward the barbed wire and fell to his knees.

Matt looked around in horror as the rain moved closer. "No chance, my friend." He lifted Tonto's arm over his shoulder.

Tanya took the other arm and they struggled toward the wire, half carrying, half dragging Tonto.

"You'll never make it," he said. "Leave me, save yourselves."

"Shut up," Tanya said. "We'll make it." They picked Tonto up and carried him. The roar of the rain on the sand behind them got louder.

But the storm lacked the power of the one the yucca plant had generated. The rain slowed finally and the clouds dissipated, spattering only a few drops on the heel of Matt's boot. The leather smoked.

They laid Tonto on the sand. Tanya knelt and brushed sand off his face. "I told you, they're not at their best after …"

"Who would be?" he said.

"Please don't say that." She walked away and stood staring at the stars.

Matt walked up behind her. "Tanya …"

She buried her face in her hands. Her shoulders shook, her words were muffled. "Elmo loved me. I just wish I could have been the woman he needed …"

"I'm sorry."

"I was never cut out to be a bartender's wife." She stared down at the sand. "Maybe in my next life …"

"You deserve another chance."

"At least I'm free. I have you to thank for that."

❧

The three sat in a circle under the stars. Baxter lay close by, muzzle on his paws, following the conversation. The Harley stood nearby, waiting like a patient horse. The desert landscape, pale under the stars, stretched beyond it to infinity.

Matt thought about his first battle with the gods. He had pictured a powerful, unstoppable enemy towering above him. Instead, he sensed weakness in Raava. He may have been mighty once, but he'd had it easy too long, spending his days like some Roman emperor, fornicating and watching his cruel entertainments, basking in the adoration of the populace he had enslaved. He was vain and he was vulnerable.

They had hiked across the sand until the blue-white glow of the crystal wall faded into darkness, but they held no illusions that they were out of harm's way. Tonto stared out into the darkness. "The gang from the White Knuckle Roadhouse are gonna be wondering what happened to Elmo," he said. "They'll likely come looking."

"I lived with Elmo at the White Knuckle for almost a year," Tanya said. "I know all those guys, I'll handle them."

"But there's only one way to handle Raava." Matt sipped the Cannon Ball Cordial, passed the bottle around.

Tonto held up the bottle. "Where did Elmo get this?"

"He cooked it up himself," Tanya said. "His granddaddy was a moonshiner."

"Cannon balls are pretty hard to come by."

"He traded with some outliers down by the river. Three horses and a deer rifle for a gunny sack of cannon balls. Set up a still behind the Roadhouse." Tanya sighed. "Elmo was trying to get me back. He loved me."

"I know how he must have felt." Matt explained the horrors of his journey through the labyrinth, the joy he felt at being in the presence of his wife's spirit. "Thought I'd lost her forever. Then I heard her voice. That's when I realized …"

Tanya studied him, concern in her face. "You may love her, but can you trust her?"

"I've always trusted her."

"She tried to set you on fire," Tonto said.

"I drove her to that." Matt said. He paced in the sand as he talked. "I broke my leg one time, lost my job. She took a second job at a drive-in to keep us from losing the house. She took care of me every night when she got home, doing things a wife should never have to do for a husband. And then, in the morning, she would get me out of bed and help me limp around the house. Physical therapy." He smiled at the memory. "I got pretty damned depressed, but then she would give me that smile, a little kiss, and just turn everything around. I love her. I love her for how she made me feel. How much she trusted me. I have to earn that trust back. I have to get her out of that place."

Tanya shrugged. "The problem is, assuming you can get back *into* the labyrinth and find her, what do you do then?"

Tonto prodded. "Need a plan, man."

"The gods are at war with each other," Matt said. "We need to fan those flames. War can be one hell of a distraction. I don't know exactly what the war is about. Whatever my wife and her mother stumbled into at Raavacon upset everything." Matt explained how his mother-in-law had died and his wife had been drawn to her grave by an irresistible force. How he had seen a hideous creature with a chrome face at the grave.

"The gods retaliating?" Tanya asked.

"I don't know, but whoever pulled me into the labyrinth didn't count on my bringing Emily's ashes with me. I think that put a kink in the system, upset the order of things somehow."

"It's all about the ashes," Tanya said. "True believers want their ashes to rest on the mountain, even though it's a sink-hole for your soul."

"My mother-in-law's ashes must be there."

Tonto nodded. "And Emily wanted to join her, but Emily's ashes are—"

"—all over my leathers."

"That's why she helped you through the labyrinth, so you could carry her ashes to the mountain."

Matt scuffed his boot in the sand. "I can't see her doing that."

"Truth is hard to hear sometimes," Tonto said.

Tanya said, "They say anyone whose ashes make it out of the labyrinth—that's never happened before—will rejoin their spirit and become whole again."

Matt jumped to his feet. "Brought back from the dead? Nobody's ever done *that* before."

"Just the one guy," she said.

"I could hold her in my arms, see that wonderful smile again. And I could get her out of there."

Tonto shook his head. "You getting out is one thing. Getting her out of there is a different story."

They huddled together in the starlight, discussing the job ahead: how to get back into the labyrinth. The most likely portal had to be somewhere near the Raavacon conference, a spot marked now only by Tonto's kiosk. That was where the original disturbance occurred. Matt had emerged from the labyrinth nearby.

They talked until exhaustion overtook them. Matt's head nodded on his chest. A sharp pain in his back prodded him awake. A rag-tag group of men surrounded them, holding clubs and broken bottles. Twelve angry men. The gang from the White Knuckle.

A thin man in a leather vest jabbed a finger at a growling Baxter. "Dog bit my nuts." He raised his club. "They're all swoled up."

A smile twisted Matt's lips. "Hey, he's a nice dog."

The big man in the black leather coat pulled Matt to his feet. "Forget the damn dog. Where's Elmo?"

"He's dead," Matt said.

"You killed him?" The big man raised Elmo's barbed-wire-wrapped fence rail.

"Put that down, Westley." Tanya uncrossed her legs and rose nimbly from the sand. "These men saved me, brought me back. Now they really need your help."

The men closed around the three travelers, a circle of silent menace.

"Elmo tried to help us," she said. "He didn't make it back."

"And now you want *us* to get involved?" Westley said. "We mess with those guys, we're dead meat." The big man nodded his head toward the border.

"You're not afraid, are you? Tonto asked.

"Damn straight."

"Little late to worry about that," Tanya said. She told them about their confrontation with Raava. How Matt had pulled her and Tonto across the border. "Raava was in a rage, sent the acid rain after us."

"Raava thinks we're all traitors," Tonto said.

Westley took a breath, exchanged glances with his cohorts. Finally nodded his head. "That means we're in it now, whether we want to be or not." Resignation in his voice.

Matt laid his hand on the big man's shoulders. "Thank you." Matt drew him away from the group. "Here's what I need you to do."

The man's eyes got wider as Matt whispered in his ear. He stepped back, shaking his head. "How long do we have to keep it up?"

"Ten, fifteen minutes. Enough to give us a head start."

The big man gathered his gang around him and they stood, heads together in a huddle. Amid a chorus of laughs, shouts and good-natured jostling, he explained the diversion Matt had requested. "Just like Hollywood," he said.

He swung a wild roundhouse at the man beside him. The man rolled into a back somersault in the sand, jumped to his feet and charged the big man. The man in the vest tripped him. Someone grabbed his club and waded into the group, swinging it over his head. Westley tackled him. Shouted curses and the fight was on.

Tanya and Tonto dashed for the Harley. Matt scooped Baxter under his arm and followed. The noise of the battle rose behind them. Someone fired a pistol in the air. Emotions running high. A perfect diversion. The three travelers stood by the bike and passed the Cannon Ball Cordial.

"Can you drink and ride?" Tanya asked. A genteel belch.

Matt gave her a lopsided grin. "No cops out here." He threw his leg over the bike. Tonto climbed on behind him, and Tanya, Baxter cradled in her arms, slid between them. The bike roared to life. Matt tipped the throttle. "Watchman, can you do that time-space continuum thing?"

Tonto shook his head. "Raava revoked my privilege. Have to go real time."

"How far is it to the Raavacon conference?"

"Depends. How fast can this thing go?"

"Let's find out."

Tanya threw her arms around Matt's waist, fingers digging into the ash-covered leather.

A rooster tail of dirt and gravel rose behind the bike. The dust cloud churned up by the faux fighters fell away behind.

CHAPTER TEN

The watchman's shack had been reduced to a scattering of broken sticks, strewn in the sand along with charred fragments of the yucca. All these artifacts decorated the rim of a gaping crater. Deep shadows at the bottom masked the crater's true depth. Baxter ran to the yucca stump and raised his leg.

"That must be the way in." Matt pointed to the crater.

Tonto and Tanya stood beside him. "You can't be serious," Tonto said.

"Dead serious. Maybe for the first time in my life," Matt said.

"I'm going with you." Tanya said. "I have god fluids in me. Vaatu can't touch me."

Tonto looked away.

"What's the matter?" she asked.

"Nothing. I just …"

She patted his hand. "I understand. I think you're sweet."

"And I think you're beautiful."

"It's the god fluids, isn't it?" She moved closer.

A reluctant nod.

"Nothing I could do about that," she said. "But you know it's not permanent."

"I was being stupid. I'm sorry. I just imagined you and him …"

"I still think you're sweet." She slid her hand into his.

"You two stay here and get acquainted," Matt said. "I've put you in danger long enough. From now on I go alone."

She grabbed Matt's arm. "I can go places you can't, Ash Man."

Matt lifted the Harley onto its stand. "I won't ask you to do that. Isn't your fight."

"I owe you. You can't make it by yourself."

"We'll see." He shouted down into the crater, "Vaatu, you are a weak, insipid piece of shit."

Tonto cringed behind the Harley. "Oh, no."

Matt fought back against the force pulling him toward the crater, legs stretched out before him, boots plowing sand. Tanya ran after him, grabbed his belt. They flew over the edge and disappeared.

⁂

They floated together in the darkness somewhere below the crater. The force was stronger here, pulling them deeper. Matt reached out, found Tanya's hand.

"You told me you drank from the river," Tanya said. "Do you know what that means?"

"Tell me."

"People believe it makes you one with the river. You draw strength from it."

"People believe a lot of things."

"You've been in this place long enough to realize there might be something beyond your science. You kicked a god in the nuts, for heaven's sake."

"Are you smiling?"

She lifted his hand to her lips. She was smiling. "What's your plan?" she said.

"Find Emily and get her out of here."

"What's your plan?" she repeated.

"Working on it."

Matt realized he could see Tanya's smile. A faint blue light coming from behind him shone on her face. Her eyes opened wide in amazement. Shimmering blue orbs floated toward them. Matt reached out to snag two, handed one to Tanya. They ate and in a moment a feeling of well-being washed over them. "Not too many," he said. "These things are potent."

A floating procession of cannon balls moved toward them through space. Then, one by one, they began to disappear. As Matt and Tanya moved closer, a pinkish light grew in the space around them. Matt made out shiny shapes flitting toward them in the darkness, pink neon tongues glowing like beacons in the darkness.

"Guardians," Tanya said.

"Chrome lizards." Sweat broke out on Matt's forehead. His jacket still bore the rips from their teeth and claws. He floated helplessly, watching their advance, snapping up the blue orbs as they came. One floated up to them, teeth flashing.

"Get back," Matt yelled.

The creature advanced, jaws snapping, almost in their faces now.

Tanya reached out a finger, touched the creature's nose. It froze in mid-bite. A school of the lizards gathered around their comrade and tore him apart in a feeding frenzy. Tanya immobilized several more and soon the darkness around them churned with flashing teeth and floating pieces of dismembered lizards. The oily red blood he had seen before in the labyrinth waved around them like seaweed. Tanya's white dress was marbled with red.

"Listen," she said. "Can you hear water?"

"Lizards making too much noise—no, I hear it."

Tanya pointed. "We need to go this way, farther in."

He shouted into the darkness, "Vaatu, you're a squatty, ugly little troll." A force pulled them free of the carnage from the chrome lizard attack, sent them moving through the darkness with gathering speed.

"Careful, we can't get too close to him," Tanya said. "You won't get away with kicking Vaatu in the balls." The stream of blue orbs had thickened now and the travelers reached out, gathering them, stuffing them in their clothes

"Jump, Ash Man."

"What about you?" he said.

"Come back and get me." She hugged him. "That's sweet. You thought about me."

Matt threw out his arms and leaped over the edge in an awkward swan dive.

Floating.

He drifted out over the canyon and felt a cooling mist from the river he had felt before. He pulled his arms back, breast-stroking in the air. Tanya stood on the edge of the precipice waving at him. He swam toward her, caught her hand and pulled her out into the air just as another blast of light tore away the rock where she had been standing. Matt swam away above the river, Tanya clinging to his shoulders.

Chapter Eleven

The river below them grew closer. The effect of the cannon balls was wearing off and fear crept over Matt. They had traveled for what seemed like miles but saw no sign of the Ice Bridge. He struggled to stay on the thin line where competing energy fields cancelled each other out, but there could be no doubt: he was being pulled down.

"Vaatu is pulling us," Tanya said. Her arms loosened around his neck, she slid backward. The stars still twinkled overhead but the canyon walls seemed to be closing in, the gap narrowing. As they drifted lower, the sound of the river got louder, a muffled roar. The cool mist touched his face and he remembered Tanya's words: "She won't let you drown."

They fell the last few feet into the water. Matt pushed her toward the shore as he went under. The current slammed his body into the rocks. He fought the urge to cry out, held his breath until finally his reflexes forced him to open his mouth, gasp for air. He took a breath, then another. He was breathing underwater

He pushed himself to the surface, smiled at Tanya treading water near the shore. "A miracle!"

She wiped water from her eyes. "I told you the river would protect you."

She held onto his shoulders as they floated on down the river. The water's roar faded, became a soft rushing sound as it slid through a flat, green meadow. Tanya slipped off Matt's back and climbed onto the soft, forgiving grass. Matt climbed out and lay down beside her. Flowering shrubs and trees surrounded them, red and yellow blossoms in profusion, their scent heavy in the air. The grass waved in the soft caresses of the water at river's edge. All was dimly lit by a narrow band of stars marking the canyon's rim.

But Matt was nervous. Nowhere in the labyrinth had he seen such an idyllic setting: Elysium. A special place— but for who? Vaatu had come at them with lightning and fire when he discovered they were in his realm. Here, all was silent and serene. Matt could not believe Vaatu had just given up. They kept a watchful eye around them as they crossed the meadow. The foliage grew thicker, the scent of flowers almost overpowering.

The peacefulness of the place, the hypnotic sound of the river, dulled their senses. "Thought the labyrinth was hell," Matt said. "This looks more like Heaven. Not that I believe in Heaven."

"Looks that way, but I—"

"I can imagine Emily stepping out of those trees, smiling at me and …"

"I've had dreams like that about Elmo," Tanya said. They walked away from the river into a shaded grotto near the rock wall where overhanging trees blocked the sky and the shadows deepened.

"I know how much you miss Elmo. I'm sorry."

"You're a kind man," Tanya said. "Emily was a lucky woman. I'd like to meet her." She hugged him.

Matt felt her warmth against him, smiled and pulled her closer. The world, it seemed, had shrunken to this grotto. He took a breath and gently pushed her away. They walked on, feet flattening the grass, leaving a meandering trail across the meadow. "Doesn't look like anyone has walked this way before," Matt said.

"Matt, the grass." Tanya stepped back from a patch of grass that had suddenly turned brown at her feet. The browning spread toward them and they backed away. Everything, bushes, flowers and grass, wilted and darkened as if suddenly exposed to a blow torch. "It's all dying." The perimeter of death spread across the meadow, killing everything in its path. Clouds gathered overhead, blotting out the stars. Light in the meadow faded. A rumble of thunder drowned out the sound of the river.

Matt and Tanya retreated until their backs were against a rock wall. The vegetation curled and blackened, sending up puffs of foul-smelling smoke. It reminded Matt of the acid rain in the desert that destroyed everything in its path. The two huddled together, shaking with fear.

A slab of rock broke away from the wall beside them and slammed down onto the blackened grass. A cloud of dust and smoke rose around it, obscuring some movement. Someone—something—stepped out. The dust drifted away and there on the smoldering slab of rock stood a slender figure with a shock of greased-back auburn hair. The figure leaned forward, scowled, eyes angry beneath severely slanted eyebrows, an expression Matt found frighteningly familiar: Larry Unger, his ninth grade math teacher.

Matt gripped Tanya's arm. "Oh, Jesus."

"Hello, Mr. Thanos. Still playing with yourself?"

Matt's teacher had died years ago from cancer, yet here he stood, still wearing baggy corduroys cinched around his hips by a green plastic belt, a wrinkled blue polo shirt hanging over a tight little watermelon belly. He'd been Matt's worst teenage nightmare.

Tanya whispered, "Vaatu."

A lifetime of suppressed memories of all the embarrassing moments in the four-year hell that had been high school boiled up, leaving Matt gasping for breath, face glowing red with embarrassment. Mr. Unger had spotted Matt rubbing his crotch in algebra class and announced it to the whole class. He'd found him with his eye plastered to a knot hole in the girl's locker room, and dragged him to the principal's office. He had been expelled, ordered off the school grounds. His cheeks burned at the memory.

Vaatu pushed coke-bottle glasses up on his nose, stared bug-eyed at Matt. "I can still see you, out behind the gym, dick dangling in the air, still damp from Linda Smither's amateur blow job. How we all laughed at that. So small."

Life, death and the challenges of the labyrinth had toughened Matt. This pathetic—hologram—could not intimidate him now. He stepped forward, chin at a belligerent angle. "You're a sadistic fuck."

"You escaped the labyrinth. Tell me how you did that."

"Kill me first, Vaatu."

"I could do that, but there are things worse than dying. You have seen them, the faceless ones, who fight and are beaten and punished for entertainment, who roam alone in darkness and terror for all eternity. You have met them, have you not? Shared their terror? You will join them."

Matt planted his hands on his hips. "You lured my wife and her mother into this crazy-cult world and now they're both lost down here in your hell."

"You accuse me of harming your mother-in-law? Foolish little man." He snapped his fingers and a hooded figure in a blood-red robe stepped out of the break in the cliff face and came to his side. The figure drew the hood back.

Matt found himself staring at Joyce, his mother-in-law. An awful clarity overcame him. He had never liked this woman; she was a nasty, vindictive shrew. Even Baxter had growled at her, if she tried to pet him. But Matt had never guessed the fullness of her evil. Never could he have imagined this: she was Vaatu's woman.

Joyce Graves arched her brow and smiled. She looked twenty years younger. Her now-blond hair was pinned into a perfect chignon, a youthful blush softened her cheeks, her breasts rode high under the velvet robe.

"It looks like you've put on a little weight. How long have you worked for this clown?" Matt asked.

Vaatu's raised hand demanded silence. "Joyce does not *work* for me. Hers is a labor of love." She shivered when he ran his hand up her arm. He frowned at Matt. "And I am not a *clown*."

"You're a bad boy, Matt," Joyce said.

"And you're a perfect bitch, Joyce." Matt shook his head, disgusted. "You traded your daughter's life for a face lift."

Vaatu stepped off the stone slab and strode across the scorched brown grass. "As fascinating as all this bickering is, there are more important items on our agenda. You escaped my labyrinth and got past my guardians. How? Did this beautiful lady have anything to do with it?" He leered at Tanya.

She hissed at him like a snake.

"A beautiful prize," Vaatu said. "Is she for me?" He touched her breast. His arm jerked spasmodically and fell away. His face contorted in anger and surprise. "You have the fluids in you!" He turned an accusing eye on Joyce. "You didn't tell me about this one. Afraid of competition?"

"You are mine. There is no competition."

Vaatu stared at Joyce until a tear leaked from the corner of her eye.

She turned away.

Two faceless men wearing leather breast plates and helmets appeared on the stone slab behind Vaatu. "I know your worst fears, Matthew Thanos. Gentlemen, remove Mr. Thanos' pants."

"Not this time, Unger." Matt lunged at Vaatu, grabbed his throat and squeezed. Unger's glasses fell off, and a wet stain appeared on his crotch. Matt glanced down, smiled. Unger twisted away, trying to hide his shame. Matt laughed. "Scared the piss out of you, did I?"

Then the math teacher was gone, replaced by a creature twice Matt's height with massive steel claws for hands. His face was a chrome rictus, framing rows of needle sharp teeth. A blue-green robe swirled around his massive thighs.

He lifted Matt by his hair, and dangled him before his two leather-clad Centurions. "Now," he thundered, "Take off his pants."

"No! Stop!" Matt cried. He felt his scalp ripping away from the top of his skull. "I'll tell you what you want to know."

Tanya grabbed his hand. "No, Ash Man. Don't give up." He felt the soft, reassuring squish of a cannon ball in his hand. He popped it in his mouth. The pain became tolerable, and a Zen-like mixture of calmness and courage flowed through him.

Vaatu stared into Matt's eyes. "Why did she call you 'Ash Man'?"

"The fluids will protect me," Tanya whispered.

Matt understood. "Just don't put me in the river," he said. "Anything but that." He raised his hands, clasped in supplication to Vaatu.

"Our little man is afraid of the water." Vaatu carried Matt by the hair across the lawn to the river, his two Centurion guards at his sides. Matt's feet dangled over the water.

His hands, still pressed together in a wedge, flashed upward in a sword hand strike at Vaatu's unprotected throat. The god gagged and reached for his neck. Matt slipped from his grasp and slid into the water.

❧

The world was a cool, murky blue-green when Matt opened his eyes. The water cooled his injured scalp. The current carried him swiftly downstream. He took a breath.

Another. A luxurious feeling of freedom, breathing under water.

His strength returned and he popped to the surface. The rock walls slipped rapidly by and he heard the sound of approaching rapids. He sank below the surface, let himself relax and flowed with the current over the rocks. At the bottom of the rapids, he floated to a pool out of the current's reach. Starlight reflected on the water's surface. The languid motion of the river brought Matt a feeling of peace.

The feeling faded as his gaze shifted upward. In the distance, a towering cone-shaped form loomed to an impossible height, blocking out the stars. The remains of all the souls who had ever lived on earth.

The Mountain of Ashes.

Chapter Twelve

Matt swam up the river from the Mountain of Ashes, staying underwater most of the way to avoid the roving patrols of chrome lizards searching for him along the bank. Finally, he surfaced and found himself at what looked like a whore house. The crude structure, hastily constructed from rocks and sticks, seemed the work of a desperate adversary. Even the sign gouged into a rotting board above the doorway lacked subtlety. *House of Joy Come in: We Never Close.* Something from a Looney Tunes cartoon.

Matt paddled to the bank, head just above the surface. He'd been in the water for what seemed like hours, but time was meaningless in this place. There was no sign now of the chrome lizards that pursued him along the banks since he'd left the mountain behind. Some had dived in after him, only to flail in panic, scramble back to shore and collapse on the bank. They seemed, probably owing to their metallic exoskeletons, deathly afraid of water. His new-found ability to breathe submerged, together with his continuous ingestion of cannon balls, had protected him on his long journey upstream. Vaatu was nowhere to be seen.

Matt's journey thus far seemed fruitless. No sign of Tanya, or the Ice Bridge. A narrow band of stars arched above the towering canyon walls. This bizarre structure before him reminded him of the White Knuckle Roadhouse, the outpost outside Raava's crystal empire. If this place had been constructed for a similar purpose, it meant that the Ice Bridge must be nearby. Though the House of Joy might be a trap, he had no choice but to spring it, whatever dangers lay inside.

The windowless parlor was furnished with cast-off chairs, all of them occupied by women lounging in lingerie of various shades of blue and purple. They all bore striking resemblances to Hollywood stars from the golden age of movies: Lana Turner, Rita Hayworth, Veronica Lake.

A narrow stairway led up from the parlor into darkness. A woman he guessed to be the madam, a dead ringer for Jayne Mansfield, sat on a green velveteen sofa petting a chrome lizard. Her blue satin nightgown slit up the side showed an expanse of pale skin and a muscular calf. The lizard hissed as Matt approached. The madam batted its head and it fell silent.

"I'm looking for a woman," Matt said. "A brunette if you have one."

She pointed up the stairs.

Matt spotted a segment of narrow elastic extending from the edge of the madam's face into her hair and realized the face she presented was a mask. His senses sprang to high alert. The women sitting around the parlor squirmed in their seats. He looked up the stairs. The trap, no doubt, awaited him there.

Matt climbed to a darkened hallway. A single door to his left hung part way open. Faint yellow light spilled into the corridor. Matt heard footsteps behind him on the stairs. He hurried to the door and peered inside, drew in a ragged breath, his eyes wide. There, on a sagging metal cot, sat Tanya, wearing a skimpy red negligee. Pale yellow light from a lamp with a fringed shade on the night stand tinted her face an unhealthy saffron color.

"I knew you'd come." She put her fingers to her lips and whispered, "It's a trap."

Matt nodded. "I know. How did you get here?"

"The men with no faces tied me up and carried me."

"I thought the god fluids protected you."

"Only from Vaatu and his spawn," she said.

"You mean the lizards? They're his 'spawn'?"

"You didn't notice the resemblance?"

"If he's the father of those things, who's the mother?"

Tanya shrugged. "The woman in the red robe?"

Shuffling footsteps in the hall interrupted their conversation. A blonde head peeked around the door. Matt reached for the mask, yanked it off. The featureless visage underneath it shone like pewter in the light from Tanya's lamp. The faceless man lashed out with a club. Matt dodged it and hooked a fist into the creature's midsection, sending him the floor.

A pair of chrome lizards scuttled in, snapping their teeth, waving their claws. Matt and Tanya hopped onto the bed. The lizards crawled after them. Tanya tapped each on their noses and they froze, immobile on the blanket.

Tanya grabbed Matt's hand and pulled him off the bed and out into the hall. "Down this way," she said, pointing to a door at the end.

Matt ran to the door and threw it open. On the other side a ribbon of ice arched up into the darkness. He recognized it immediately. "The Ice Bridge."

"What do we do?" Tanya asked.

The ice was too steep and slick to climb by hand. "Stay here. I'm going to get the lizards."

❧

Matt grabbed the two lizards off the bed and carried them back down the hall. He slammed the two immobilized reptiles against the ice, claws and teeth forward. The sharp metal bit into the glossy surface. Lizard crampons. *Work with what you got.* He tugged on them, testing their grip. "How long before they come back to life?"

"A few minutes, an hour, I don't know," she said. "I've never stuck around long enough to find out."

Matt heard a clatter of claws in the hallway. More of the creatures scuttled towards them. Tanya tapped two of them, picked them up and swung them hard against the ice as Matt had. A squad of the faceless men lock-stepped toward them down the hall, still wearing their movie star masks, arms locked in the line formation Matt had seen them use at the Game.

"Go," Matt screamed. He and Tanya struggled up the ice. Clubs beat against the ice around them, sending shards flying. Matt and Tanya scrambled upward out of reach.

The bridge arched over the river. The monsters Matt had seen on his last crossing reappeared, the alligators, the armadillos. They were joined now by hideous leather-winged birds with ruby eyes that dove at them and swerved away into the darkness. Matt's rational mind said the creatures could not be real, but he scrambled frantically upward, eyes closed, arms strained to the breaking point.

The river, a strip of silver far below, seemed a symbol of strength and a source of comfort. He took deep breaths, imagined himself drifting in its cooling depths. He forced himself to relax, called to Tanya, who labored a few feet below him: "Crossing the Ice Bridge is a journey not only of the body, but of the mind."

A huge orange cobra curled down the ice toward them, tongue flicking. Tanya recoiled in horror, lost hold of her paralyzed lizards and grabbed Matt's ankle. The cobra bared its fangs and slid toward them. Matt pried one of his lizards off the ice and hurled it at the snake. The reptile's fangs sunk into the lizard's body. The snake stiffened, swayed for a moment and toppled off the bridge.

Matt flattened himself against the slippery surface and closed his eyes. Vertigo tightened his bowels. He slid back, dug in his boot toes. They were near the crest of the arch, where the slope was shallower. He managed to stop his slide. Tanya, pulling on his pants and jacket, scrambled up beside him.

They groped and clawed their way up the last several feet to the crest of the bridge and stopped, gasping for breath. Tanya's head drooped with exhaustion. She shivered from the cold. After a brief rest, they started down the gentler downward slope, approaching an array of glowing curtains, quivering sheets of light fading from gold to silver to green.

They reached the bottom, stood up and stepped off the ice. Tanya was shaking now, stumbling forward, eyes closed. "… sleepy … lie down."

Matt unzipped his leather jacket, pulled her close and wrapped it around them both. He picked her up and carried her through the glowing curtains into the darkness of a cave beyond.

He had reentered the labyrinth. The air was still, the silence pressed on him like a weight. Fear again quickened his breath. But this time he was not alone. Together, he and Tanya would face whatever horrors lay beyond in the darkness. Guilt tugged at him. She had done nothing to deserve being in this awful place. She was here for his sake. Now he must care for her.

He dug in his pocket for a cannon ball and held it to her lips. She chewed and swallowed. They lay down on the stones. He pulled her against him. After a few moments, he felt her body grow warmer. She curled into him. He brushed her hair back from her forehead, kissed her cheek and let her sleep, listening for Emily's voice in the darkness.

Chapter Thirteen

Matt and Tanya felt their way along a rock wall guided only by the faint luminescence of their last cannon ball. They had stumbled for hours through featureless caverns, followed a dozen branching tunnels, seen and heard nothing. The air seemed warmer now. The cannon ball's glow faded. Darkness closed in around them.

Deafening silence.

A line from his religious youth came to Matt: "Cast into outer darkness." All the fears that had haunted him before returned. Trapped forever, blind and helpless. He stumbled ahead, clutching Tanya's hand, breath rasping in his throat, sweat running down his body. A terrible thirst built in his throat. They would have to find water soon.

A soft light, whose source was not immediately apparent, blossomed around them. A face framed in flowing red hair hovered in the air. The image was faint, as if diffused through gauze, but it was unmistakably Emily.

"Who is this?"

"A friend."

"I can see that by the way she's dressed."

Tanya grasped Matt's hand. "I'm Tanya. We're just friends."

"Sure."

"It's a long story," Matt said.

"You deserted me, left me alone in the dark. I was terrified."

"Deserted you? You practically threw me off the Ice Bridge," Matt said.

"He loves you," Tanya called out. "He risked his life to come back for you."

"Is that true? You came back for me?"

"There's a way to get you out of here," Matt said.

"Aren't you forgetting I'm dead?"

"Dead seems to be relative here. I found out that if your spirit and your ashes are reunited, you can get back your original body—reanimated. I have your ashes. I've come back for your spirit—for you."

"Even if that were true, what are we supposed to do, just walk out the door? This is Vaatu's domain."

A low thunder, felt more than heard, filled the cavern. The floor shook, sending Matt and Tanya sprawling on the rocks. The roar got louder. They covered their ears.

"What the hell …" Emily said.

Tanya shouted, "Raava and Vaatu are fighting."

"Why?"

"They've been fighting a cold war for millennia," Tanya said. "Whatever happened at Raavacon pushed things to the boiling point."

"What did happen at Raavacon?" Matt asked.

"Mother got me to distract the guards while she snuck into the Inner Council meeting."

"Why would she do that?"

"She was seeking the truth."

Matt kept his expression neutral. "Did she find it?"

"I never found out."

"What happened?"

"I saw a flash of light. The floor shook and the corridor filled up with smoke. A creature appeared wearing a white robe. A skeleton face, empty eye sockets. I still see that face when I close my eyes."

"An angel?"

"Not hardly. I can still see his bloody hands reaching for me, smell his breath—like rotten meat. I went into hysterics and passed out. My mother dragged me out of there. She saved my life."

"You never told me about this."

"I was still in shock when we got home. You'd have laughed your ass off."

Matt nodded. "There was a time …"

"It was the evil one—in the flesh."

"The evil one? That's what your mother told you?"

"Yes, Vaatu."

"You're on the wrong side of history," Matt said. "Your mother is a *spy* for Vaatu."

"How could that be true? And how could you know this?"

"Let's just say we ran into her along the way." Matt heard the tramp of marching feet echo up through the cavern. "I'll explain later. I think we better keep moving."

Faceless men appeared out of the gloom, swinging clubs, marching toward them ten abreast. Tanya pulled at Matt. "Vaatu's thugs, looking for us."

Matt nodded. "We have to get out of here."

"We? What about me?" Emily said.

"I'll come back for you, but I have to live long enough to do it. Will you help?"

"How?"

"Throw a fit. Get angry, yell, curse," Matt said.

"What good will that do?"

Matt rolled his eyes in exasperation. He didn't have time to deal with Emily's stubbornness. "Just do it, moron," he said. That worked.

"Moron?" Emily's ghostly face contorted with rage. *"You're the moron, you selfish, egotistical asshole!"* Her voice rose. She was screaming now, cursing, calling him names he hadn't heard since boot camp. But she aimed her ire at Vaatu's faceless minions. Matt smiled. She had understood his strategy. He and Tanya closed their eyes,

sat cross-legged against the wall, slowed their breathing and cleared their minds.

The faceless men broke formation and milled around, pounding their clubs against the walls and the ceiling. Matt heard a thump as a body fell near him, apparently the victim of a cohort's club.

"You're so goddamn dumb you probably can't see that hole in the wall down to your left," Emily interrupted her rant to whisper.

Matt and Tanya crept along the wall, slipping past the flailing soldiers. It was a tight squeeze, but they made it into the hole and struggled up a slanting, tubular passage. Ahead, the rush of falling water played a soft counterpoint to the rolling thunder of the god-wars overhead. Emily's image rematerialized in the blackness before them. She was smiling. *"Like old times, huh?"*

Matt smiled back. "We were always big on teamwork."

The passage opened up. Tanya got to her feet and walked ahead. "The river is right here," she said. "Water is really cold."

Matt felt for her hand in the dark. "It might be our way out."

"You can't leave me alone." Emily's voice shook with fear.

"Have to," Matt said.

"Why?"

"We're going to find Vaatu, provoke him, drive him into a frenzy, and then do the same with Raava. They tear each other apart and we bring down this whole house of cards. Then I can come back and get you out."

"I thought you were trying to survive!"

"I am. We are. I know it sounds crazy, but please trust me. I'll come back, I promise." He waded knee-deep into the stream. "Tanya, get on my back, put your arms around my neck."

"Are you sure about this?" she asked.

"No."

Tanya climbed on. Her red negligee trailed across the water. He made a shallow dive and disappeared under the surface.

The current took them.

❧

Emily's tearful specter hovered over the rushing water, watching Matt and Tanya float away. "I'll be lost in here forever." Her mind reeled with the thought of her mother's duplicity. What Matt had told her couldn't possibly be true. Her mother in concert with the Evil One? But what if Matt was right?

"Mother."

Silence.

A scream: "Mother!"

More silence.

Hysterics would solve nothing. Emily stared down at the water, mesmerized by the rhythmic shimmer.

Barely a whisper: "Mom?"

But her mother was not coming back. Only the soft sound of the water. She was alone. No choice but to trust Matt Thanos. Her future—for all eternity—was in his hands.

Chapter Fourteen

The river cascaded off the rocks, falling at frightening speed. Tanya clung to Matt's back as they swept over a series of waterfalls, gliding finally into a channel in the canyon floor. Stars shone overhead, dimmed by clouds of dust from the battle. They were out of the labyrinth, passing under the thin, glowing arc of The Ice Bridge.

The current slowed. They swam to the bank and climbed out.

"I hate to admit it," Matt said. "But I am completely lost."

"We're on the Gravity Frontier that runs down the middle of the river," Tanya said. "It ends at the Mountain of Ashes." This, she went on to explain, was the most dangerous part of the underworld, a contested area where neither god held sway. This zone separated the labyrinth, Vaatu's stronghold, from the crystal kingdom where Raava ruled.

"Like the Gaza strip," Matt said.

"Well, there's a desert in the middle but that's where the similarity ends."

"Time and space are fluid on the desert," Matt said.

"How do we find Vaatu in all this *fluidity*?" she asked.

"We call him out. He'll pull us to him, like he did at the crater."

"And then he's got us. This is not a good plan."

"You forgot our secret weapon," Matt said. "Cannon balls. We have to go get more." He leaned his head back, cupped his hands into a megaphone and shouted, "Vaatu, you're a stupid clown. Ugly on top of that. Your face looks like a mouse peeking out of a horse's ass."

Tanya raised an eyebrow. Matt shrugged.

Immediately, a force pulled at him, dragging him across the grass. He grabbed Tanya's hand and they drifted in the air above the river and moved downstream crossing a moonscape of steep ridges and barren valleys. Flies drawn into the spider's web—on purpose.

After a while, a rectangle of white broke the barren gray landscape. "Is that a tent?" Tanya asked.

They swooped lower. Ranks of faceless men stood around the tent, clubs at the ready. One side of the tent was open, the canvas rolled up. Tables laden with potions and ointments lined the interior. In the center sat an overstuffed recliner. A woman in a red robe stood beside it, bandaging the head of Matt's ninth grade math teacher, Larry Unger.

"Vaatu takes human form to relate to humans," Tanya said.

"Why does he have to keep taking that particular fucking form?" Matt sighed. "Looks like he lost the first battle."

Matt and Tanya drifted down behind a low hillock fifty yards away. Their feet sank into soft gray ashes.

The faceless guards stood arm in arm, forming a cordon around the tent.

"What now?" Tanya said. "Any closer and we get noticed."

"First, we replenish our cannonball supply, then we sneak in there, grab Joyce and feed her some disinformation," Matt whispered. "The goal is to make Vaatu crazy."

"It scares the shit out of me," Tanya said, "but I like it."

Faint voices from the tent: "The fighting will end soon. It *has* to end, before ..." Vaatu's stentorian voice sounded strange coming from Larry Unger's flaccid lips.

Tanya said, "What did Vaatu mean, 'The fighting *has* to end'? Before what?"

"I've got an idea, but we have to get closer," Matt said. "We need more cannon balls."

They felt the force pulling them back toward the tent as they slogged across the foothills toward the mountain. They leaned away from it—gravity like a negative wind. The hills were getting steeper. Finally, the mountain rose in front of them.

A group of shadows passed over them and they ducked instinctively. The shadows materialized into a squadron of white-robed figures flying toward the mountain in a loose formation. Each clutched a round, white stone in their hand. A line of faceless men ran over the hill and swung their clubs at the white-robed warriors. The white stones, thrown with surprising force, found their targets and several faceless men fell head-first into the ashes. Their comrades, airborne now, leather vests gleaming in the starlight, swung their clubs wildly. White-robed soldiers fell to earth like broken birds.

"We're in the war zone," Tanya said.

Matt shook his head. "Sticks and stones."

A faceless man fell into the ashes at Tanya's feet, head bashed in, brains oozing "Wow, these guys play hardball."

"No, they don't," Matt said. "Hardball is a *game*."

Puffs of ash spurted out higher up the slope, signs of the battle raging there. No way to tell who might be winning. For Matt, victory would only come if both sides lost. Only total collapse of this eerie, insane world could set Emily free.

More fighters, legions of them now, flew from all points on the compass, darting across the sky, flailing at each other under the starry sky.

Closer to the ground, clusters of shimmering blue orbs floated past. Matt and Tanya gathered as many as they could, filling their pockets.

Energized by a fresh infusion of cannon balls, they worked out their strategy as they drifted toward Vaatu's tent, letting the force pull them forward this time. They settled back in their eavesdropping post behind the hillock and peeked over the top.

Joyce again: "Why are you worried about the mountain coming down? That's Raava's evil enterprise. It has nothing to do with us."

"This is war. War is men's business."

Joyce raised an admonishing finger. "War is everybody's business."

Matt and Tanya exchanged glances. "*Raava's* evil enterprise?" he whispered. Apparently, Joyce believed Vaatu had nothing to do with the soul-mining of the Mountain of Ashes. "A chink in Vaatu's armor," Matt whispered. "Dissension in the ranks."

"Vaatu's perfect in Joyce's eyes. What would she do if she knew the truth?"

Matt said, "Let's find out."

Most of Vaatu's guards were gone, sent to the front. Larry Unger (it was hard to think of him any other way) sat up on the recliner, sipping from a copper goblet. Joyce rubbed his bandaged leg.

Tanya crept toward the tent. Two faceless guards stood motionless, clubs held across their chests, as she slipped around them.

Vaatu, however, dropped his goblet as Tanya stepped into the tent. "Guards!" he shouted.

Joyce brandished a knife.

"Wait. Hear me." Tanya waved her hand to distract them. The tent wall rose behind them. Matt peeked inside.

"Where is the Ash Man?" Vaatu demanded. "He insults me. He must pay."

"I think you have bigger troubles today. I can help you with that. I lived in Raava's domain for a time. In his very bed chamber. I learned things that could help you defeat him. Strategy, tactics."

Vaatu leaned forward, attention focused on Tanya. "You're offering to tell me these things? Why?"

Matt was inside the tent now, creeping closer.

"Revenge," Tanya said through gritted teeth. "Raava took me by force, turned me into his slave," she said. "He killed my beloved. I hate him."

"How dramatic," Vaatu said. He shot a glance at Joyce standing beside the table. She picked up a rag and a flask of clear liquid.

Tanya backed away.

Vaatu climbed out of the recliner, stumbled, then steadied himself. "You're not a convincing liar, lovely one."

Joyce doused the rag and moved toward Tanya. Matt's leather-clad arm circled her throat. He grabbed the rag and pressed it over her face. In a moment, Joyce went limp in his arms. Vaatu shouted a curse and reached for him.

Tanya jumped between. Vaatu swung his fist at her but his hand sprang away. He tripped across the recliner clutching his useless arm, cursing under his breath as he struggled to right himself.

"Run, Tanya," Matt shouted.

She backed out of the tent and ran across the ashes toward the hillock where they had hidden. Matt dragged the unconscious Joyce out the back of the tent. Her head hung down, red robe tangled around her legs. Her heels plowed furrows in the ash. The faceless men stood riveted at their posts.

Tanya ran, floundering knee-deep in ashes, thinking only of escape. Then she was on hard-packed sand, racing at top speed. When the White Knuckle Roadhouse floated over the horizon she realized her mistake. She had gone too far from the Gravity Frontier, into Raava's world. As Matt had said, time and space were fluid on the desert.

Almost at once, she felt Raava's horizontal gravity grip her and she stumbled across the sand, dragging her feet in a futile attempt to resist, growing weaker as she went. She had eaten her last cannon ball.

A familiar voice boomed across the desert. "My lovely Tanya. You decided to come back to me." Raava laughed, a bellowing, raucous shout. "Not that you had any choice."

His force pulled her inside the Road House. The bar was deserted, dust on the tables. The loneliness of the place only underscored Elmo's absence. A quiet sob escaped her lips.

She'd only been there a moment when Raava, wearing his blue-green ceremonial robes, crashed through the weathered walls and strode toward her. His sandals sent up puffs of dust. "I want the woman, the spy he sent into my camp. You have been in his domain. I know you've seen her. Where is she?"

Tanya backed away from the god. "I will tell you on one condition. My freedom."

He stood before her, legs spread, hands on hips. "You make no conditions. You will give me everything I want. Kneel."

Tanya shook her head, arms crossed defiantly over her chest. He grabbed her hair, dragged her outside and threw her onto the sand. "I've been at war all day. I deserve some relief." He loosened his sash.

Tanya closed her eyes, forced herself to relax, and reached for Raava. A dog barking in the distance, and the rumble of a motorcycle's engine distracted him. Raava opened his eyes, his erotic spell broken, and narrowed his gaze at the interloper.

Tonto slid the bike to a stop at the top of the hill. "Blow jobs in broad daylight. Your subjects would love to hear about that. Let her go."

Raava turned his attention back to Tanya. "Faster," he demanded. His eyes rolled back in his head and his legs shook. Then his eyes popped open, his face twisted into a mask of pain. He let out a roar of rage and bent over, clutching himself.

Tanya climbed to her feet and ran toward Tonto. Horizontal Gravity caught her and dragged her back toward her tormentor. Raava pinned her arms and held her to him. She watched helpless as a black cloud materialized over the desert. Thunder shook the ground. "Run, Tonto!"

He revved up the motorcycle and raced down the hill toward her. A wall of dark water pursued him, churning up the sand, vaporizing clumps of sagebrush. He goosed the big bike up on its back wheel. Tanya broke free and jumped aside. Tonto aimed the motorcycle at Raava's chest. Raava dodged, stumbled back and fell on the sand. Tanya ran.

Tonto swung the bike in a circle and raced back toward the fallen god. He spun out and lost a fateful moment righting the bike. The rain was upon him. A second before the toxic deluge hit, Tonto stood up on the pegs, raised both middle fingers in a final, futile, gesture of rebellion. He screamed a curse, the sound cut off as his body dissolved into glowing, greenish slime. The Harley's tires exploded and the bike sank into a shimmering puddle of metal.

"A brave fool," Raava said.
A flash of light and he was gone.
Thunder rolled away across the desert.

Chapter Fifteen

Matt had taken Joyce close to the Gravity Frontier, where the two gods' forces opposed each other in delicate balance. The air around him hummed with energy, threatening to tear him apart. He couldn't survive here long. Neither, it seemed, could Joyce.

She sprawled at the base of a Joshua tree, tears running down her cheeks, the ragged hem of her robe hiked above her knees. Her chest heaved as she fought for breath. Her face was a mask of misery and disgust. She threw her legs open and Matt turned away in revulsion. Grey, fleshy blobs plopped to the ground from her groin. Metal teeth bit through placental sacks and chrome lizards, twenty, thirty, or more, lay in a squirming heap between her legs. She fell onto her back, exhausted. The tiny lizards skittered away in all directions across the sand. Matt jumped out of their way.

All he could manage was, "Are you all right?"

Joyce sat up, drew a ragged breath. "Happens every so often. Downside of cohabitating with a god. I'll be all right."

"Eat this." Matt held out a luminescent blue sphere.

"What is it?"

"You'll like it."

She sniffed. "Smells like almonds. Are you trying to poison me?"

"Eat it, keep your strength up."

Joyce bit into the cannon ball. "Tastes like sushi." She swallowed. A smile crept across her face. "You're trying to get me high."

He handed her another. "How long have you been spying for Vaatu?"

She swallowed it. "Ages. Beyond time. You know, I'm feeling better."

"Beyond time? Come on."

"I told you, mock the gods at your peril. He'll destroy you."

"Not if he can't find me."

"He will. He's all-powerful. He sees everything."

Matt pulled a cannon ball from his pocket, popped it in his mouth. "Not quite. Control your emotions well enough and you become invisible," he said.

"Who fed you that crap? You'll feel his power very soon."

Matt tipped his head back and shouted, "Vaatu is weak, he's vain and he's a stupid loser." He stretched the last word into a yodel.

Joyce tilted her head, listening. The faint hum of the force fields, the whisper of the wind across the desert. No sound of an infuriated god striding forth. She frowned.

"So where is he?" Matt said.

"You won't hear him coming."

"I doubt that. He's too fond of making an entrance." He squatted in front of Joyce. "You killed your daughter."

"How can you say that? I gave her hope. I told her she could join me on the Mountain of Ashes and that we would dwell together in peace forever."

"The force pulling her into the cemetery, where did that came from?"

"Vaatu, of course. I missed my daughter so much I asked for his help."

"He underestimated the force? Come on. So you killed her by proxy."

"You and Emily were in a rage. Your feelings were so strong, both of you. You were easy to control."

"There was no body in your crypt, was there?"

"It's a portal to the labyrinth. I came here to be with Vaatu, but I'll join her on the mountain someday."

"She's not on the mountain. She's in the labyrinth," Matt said.

"She wouldn't be if you'd done what you were supposed to do."

"She wouldn't be dead if it weren't for you, Matt said. "What the hell were you trying to accomplish at Raavacon?"

"Fuck you." Joyce struggled to sit up.

"You killed her."

Joyce spit into the sand. "You're a lying shit."

"I didn't realize how much I loved her," Matt said, "until she was gone. When she finally told me what you did at Raavacon I realized none of this was her fault. It's *your* fault that she still has nightmares about the creature in the white robe. She was a different person after Raavacon. But I have a chance now to get the old Emily back."

"You won't take her away from me."

"She'll wander alone in there forever unless I can get her out."

"Nobody has ever escaped the labyrinth in all the world's history."

"I did. A lot of things have happened lately that have never happened before. See this dust on my leathers? It never washes off. There must be some kind of power in the human soul."

"What do you mean?'

"These are your daughter's ashes."

Joyce stared at his sleeve in horror. "My god, no."

"Vaatu probably never told you, if a person's ashes enter the labyrinth and don't get put on the Mountain of

Ashes, they can be transported back across the river to the upper world. That's what I'm going to do with Emily."

"Vaatu will never let you do that." Her eyes were slits. A viper.

"Maybe," Matt said. "Right now he's got a war on his hands. I suspect things are going to get a lot worse."

"Vaatu is a mighty warrior. He will never stop until all of Raava's armies are defeated."

"What if it goes the other way?"

"Unthinkable. Vaatu represents everything that's good. And good always triumphs."

Matt stared at her. "You really chugged the Kool-Aid, didn't you."

"Excuse me?"

"Do you want to touch your daughter's ashes?" A hardened gray paste covered his arm.

Joyce threw herself backward, heels dug into the sand. "Get away from me."

"She's trapped, Joyce. She'll be trapped forever unless you help me free her."

"You'll steal her from me. You always tried to do that."

"You know that Raava has millions of warriors," Matt said. "They're flying this way. Vaatu will fall."

"I feel dizzy." Joyce's head lolled back. "You're telling me it's a sneak attack?"

"Somebody should warn him."

"Warn him … yes." The cannon balls had taken effect. Joyce's face went slack, her eyelids drooped. The baby lizards had disappeared over the rolling dunes. Matt picked her up in his arms and started across the desert.

Time on the desert wavered and bent—a mirage shimmering into the distance. Matt wasn't sure how far he traveled, carrying Joyce across his back, retracing his steps into Vaatu's domain. Finally he rested on a low hummock, watching Vaatu's tent. Joyce dozed beside him.

Tanya's footprints led away across the ashes into the desert. He called to her. No response. She was hunted by *both* gods, now. Matt had no illusions that she could have survived.

A voice in his head: *"Matt?"*

Tanya! *"Hello, Ash Man."*

"How did you find me?

"Feelings are power here," she said. *"Yours were pretty strong—like a beacon. I'm flattered."*

"Where are you?"

"Raava caught me. He's holding me—my body—captive in his bed chamber."

"Your body?"

"He means to punish me as only he can do. As soon as he's able."

"He's not able?"

"When you helped me escape he was furious, but he still lusted for me so he was willing to forgive my treachery. But the last thing I did he could not forgive." She explained their sexual encounter on the desert.

"Ouch," Matt said.

"He's still recovering."

"There's a way we can set you free from Raava. Give him too much else to think about. Can you give him a message?"

"What message?"

"Tell him Vaatu is massing his forces, the faceless men, the lizards, the monsters of the Ice Bridge. An all-out assault. Tell him there's no way he can stand up to the mighty Vaatu."

"He'll never believe me."

Matt smiled. "We'll make him believe."

"How do we do that?"

"Tell him we've captured a spy, the woman he's been looking for. Tell him he can *persuade* her to tell him what Vaatu is up to."

"Poor woman. Looks like she's in pretty bad shape."

"You don't know the half of it." Matt told her about the chrome lizard births.

"I can't think about that."

"Joyce thinks Raava is coming with a million white-robed warriors. She'll tell him he's no match for the mighty Vaatu and all his legions."

"You fed her that story."

"Guilty."

"Things will explode," Tanya said. *"It'll be 'war on.'"*

"Counting on it."

Vaatu's tent flap hung motionless in the starlight. His faceless guards lay on the sand nearby, leather armor scarred and tattered. Casualties of war. Soon, if Matt could fan the flames of war between the two gods, there would be more.

He patted Joyce's cheek, shook her shoulders. She opened a bleary eye. "I brought you home," he said. He untied her and pointed at Vaatu's tent. "Ask him why he's fighting over the mountain, if it's Raava's enterprise."

Joyce stumbled bow-legged down the hill, trailing the tattered hem of her robe. The tent burst upward, canvas scattering in all directions. A figure, twice Matt's height, leaped up, remnants of canvas clinging to his shoulders. He snatched the canvas away with a steel-taloned hand and flashed gleaming chrome teeth. His bulging chest was festooned with the trappings of war, crossed bands of leather fastened with brass rivets, lower body sheathed in chrome. His armor twinkled in the starlight. Larry Unger was gone. Vaatu was going to war.

Matt watched, fascinated, from the crest of the hill.

Joyce stood before her god on wobbly legs. She clutched at his arm. "Raava is coming. Millions of warriors."

Vaatu brushed her aside. "Get out of my way."

"But you don't have to fight. You have no stake—"

"Not now, woman."

"I'm trying to warn you."

He shoved her away. She fell in the ashes.

"You're welcome," she said.

He stepped over her, kicking up clouds of ash that settled on her prostrate form. His mistress lay forgotten before the imperatives of war. His guttural war cry echoed as he soared away toward the mountain.

Joyce raised her hand in supplication to the sky, "Take me with you." Her voice was faint, but her eyes burned with anger.

Chapter Sixteen

Matt and Joyce marched together through the sagebrush, hands tied behind them. A convoy of outriders, denizens of the White Knuckle Roadhouse, rode in loose formation around them, rusted-out bikes and ATVs stirring up dust. The wreckage of the roadhouse lay scattered on the sand around them.

"Why do they get to ride and I have to walk?" Joyce's hair was matted with dust. Tears washed rivulets down her cheeks. Her robe, stained and ash-covered, flapped around her knees. She sniffled. Westley, riding nearby on his ATV, reached over and wiped her nose with his scarf.

"Thank you," she said

"We're prisoners," Matt said. "Raava's outriders captured us."

"Damn right. Bringing you in." Westley winked and popped a cannon ball into his mouth. "Don't try nothin'."

The riders fixed their faces in menacing grimaces. A thin man in a cowboy hat rode alongside Matt and slapped the back of his head. "Damn right,"

Matt shook his head. "Don't overact."

"Overact? Why are they pretending?" Joyce asked. "What's going on?"

"It's a way to get inside the crystal palace."

"The enemy camp," Joyce said.

"You're having second thoughts?"

Joyce trudged through the sand, eyes downcast. "He left me, went off to fight in a silly war. He never really cared about me."

"You wonder why Vaatu is so interested in the Mountain of Ashes. You're starting to wonder if I'm right, that it's the source of his power, too. He and Raava are birds of a feather, draining the souls of the dead to power their empires, exploiting everyone. Including you."

"Not me. He loves me."

"Right, that's why he tossed you out of his way. Help us destroy him, Joyce. He deserves it, after the way he treated you."

"He means well. He just has his mind on the war."

"You don't believe that."

She walked in silence. Matt could tell she was thinking. Finally, she said, "I'm a prisoner, what can I do?"

"Remember how you told Vaatu that Raava was massing an army against him?"

"Vaguely."

"I want you to tell Raava the same thing."

She sighed. "Set them against each other."

Matt nodded. "The battle will be cataclysmic. It will bring the Mountain down."

Joyce nodded. "Bring the bastard down." She threw her shoulders back; anger flashed in her eyes. "He left me lying in the dirt."

This was classic Joyce, Matt realized. Her first thought was vengeance at any sign of rejection. She had infused Emily with that spirit. It had served neither of them well.

—❧—

Over the hill appeared the shimmering world of crystal and glass. It sat on the shore of an endless blue sea. Westley got off his ATV and pushed a cannon ball into Matt's mouth. A layer of fog formed between glass and sand.

The big man nudged Matt and Joyce forward. They stepped through the fog bank and into the city. Joyce stared about in wonder. The streets were empty again. Matt headed for the stadium, following the roar of the crowd.

Every seat was filled. Hundreds more of Raava's white-robed subjects had spilled out onto the field. Raava pushed his way through them, batting them aside. His robe rumpled, the sash untied, his groin swathed in a layer of cotton, swaddling his injured manhood. His subjects crowded around him, some fighting to keep the smiles off their faces. Raava's power over them was faltering. His glamour was wearing off. He snarled at them. They moved back.

Joyce strode down the ramp onto the field, a wall of mirrors on each side of her reflecting her image out to infinity. The crowd fell silent.

"I can't see you, Ash Man, but I know you're here," Raava said. "Who is this woman?"

"Vaatu's spy," Matt said.

"I just heard a disturbing rumor. Supposedly my nemesis is marching on the mountain with all his legions. What say you, spy?"

"Vaatu will destroy you," Joyce spit on the glass surface of the arena. "His forces are all-powerful. You cannot stand against him."

Matt looked away to hide his smile. Joyce had missed her calling as an actress.

Raava stalked toward her, standing straighter now. He seemed to have regained his strength. He threw off the cotton wrap, retied his sash and thrust out his chest. "I am all-powerful. My forces are already defeating him on the mountain. There are thousands more here waiting to join the battle."

"Are you sure they're with you?" Matt gestured at the growing crowd of white-robed warriors. Some looked away, guilt in their faces.

"They are loyal to Raava to the end. Together, we will conquer Vaatu—once and for all."

Joyce breathed heavily, visibly agitated. She shouted at the crowd. "Your god is a liar and a fornicator. He has no honor. He feeds off your ancestors. Takes their spirits and their souls for his own glory." Her voice dropped in disillusionment: "Vaatu is no different."

People looked at each other, puzzled. Mumbled conversations drifted among them.

"This woman is the devil's messenger," Raava shouted. "Pay her no attention."

An answering shout came from a crystal arch above the stadium: "Pay attention to *me*."

The crowd turned in unison to face this new distraction.

Tanya staggered down the ramp, her red negligee torn and soiled, a purple bruise under her eye. The wall of mirrors magnified her degradation. "Here's what your sanctimonious leader does to satisfy his carnal appetites. He took me captive, forced me to—" She bit back tears. "He beat me."

"You will learn to obey." Raava pointed an accusing finger. Matt caught the slight trembling.

He called to Raava, "This little embarrassment could do you some damage. We can put an end to that. I have a deal for you."

"Deal?" Raava frowned at him.

"A trade. Vaatu's spy here in exchange for Tanya."

"You are a fool, Ash Man. You can hide behind the forbidden fruit, but nothing prevents me from killing both of these women."

Joyce shouted, "You don't have the balls."

Raava jabbed a gloved finger at her. "You won't speak that way to *me*."

Tanya pushed her way through the crowd. "You can't kill me, Raava. I'm already dead." She raised a glass dagger, held it for a dramatic moment, then plunged it into her chest. Blood, a shade darker than her negligee, spurted out, ran down her chest. The crowd fell back.

Matt rushed to her, cradled her in his arms. "Why, Tanya?"

"There is no hope for me here, only torment. I had my second chance. I'm going to the mountain to join my love, my kindred soul."

"Elmo?"

"The Watchman, Tonto. Raava caught up with him. He died trying to protect me. He and I will be together—at peace—forever."

"He was a brave man. Gave his life for you. The ultimate sacrifice, but ..."

She frowned at Matt. "Don't look at me that way. I know you may not approve of me and Tonto, but Elmo would have wanted me to be happy."

Matt's heart dropped. If the mountain were destroyed, there might never be peace. Would any of them ever be happy? He whispered, "In peace, forever." Tanya closed her eyes and went limp in his arms. Several white-robed women came forward and knelt beside her, heads bowed. They picked her up and, faces sorrowful, carried her out of the stadium.

Raava laughed. "A loss, but I expect I'll find a replacement soon."

"You see what a monster he is?" Joyce screamed, fists clenched. "He uses women and destroys them."

The mutterings from the crowd grew louder. Tanya's bearers entered the stadium in a solemn procession carrying her body aloft on a crystal slab. Matt watched in silence until the procession disappeared behind a column of mirrors, then dropped his eyes, fighting to hide his tears.

Raava roared at the crowd, "Go back to your homes."

Joyce pulled Matt aside. "Do you remember Achilles heel?"

"His fatal flaw. I know my mythology."

"Vaatu has one, too. I probably won't have another chance to tell you." She leaned closer and whispered in his ear.

His eyes widened. "That's outrageous.' he said.

"He's never told anyone."

He laid his hand on her shoulder. "Thank you."

Raava sprang forward, picked Joyce up by the arm and held her, feet dangling, above the glass boulevard.

"Get him," Joyce cried. "He can't control all of you. He is too weak."

Raava wrapped his free hand around her neck and squeezed. Sparks radiated off her body, she convulsed. Smoke rose from the folds of her robe. In a second she was a cinder. Raava threw her remains on the ground. The people closed the circle around him. Matt's voice echoed across the glass landscape. "This is the creature you've chosen as your god?"

Raava towered over his subjects now, tall as a three-story building, brandishing a sword, wearing a horned helmet and chain mail, steel boots and an ivory codpiece. "Ash Man, where are you?"

Matt shouted, "This thing is no god; he's a poser, using the souls of the dead to glorify himself. He deserves your contempt, not your adoration."

The crowd closed in on Raava. Some shook their fists.

Raava raised the sword and unleashed a high, wavering war cry. Many cringed and covered their ears. "I will deal with this infidel." He swung his sword in a slashing arc above the crowd. They held their ground. The terrible sword found no target. He swung again. Someone in the crowd gasped. The fog bank swirled along the border, the sound of motorcycle engines and ATVs. The Ash Man was gone.

Raava stomped on Joyce's ashes and scowled at the crowd. "You are with me or you are dead."

Solar wind ruffled the sea of white robes as Raava's soldiers flew in formation, toward the Mountain of Ashes, carrying their round white stones. The caravan, with Raava at its head, was miles wide. From the cloud-shrouded peak the robes flowed like a vertical ocean.

Chapter Seventeen

The entrance to the labyrinth had changed. The sign over the whorehouse entrance hung by a single wire, swinging in the solar wind. The Ice Bridge had melted loose from its moorings and swung in a gentle arc a mile above the river. Matt stepped onto it and edged his way out over the chasm. The monsters he had seen before were gone. Off to war, he supposed. The stars overhead were dimmed by dust and ash.

When his weight set the bridge swinging, he dropped to his hands and knees and crept forward. The glowing curtains were still in place at the far end but they seemed dimmer, as if the labyrinth was on emergency back-up power, depleted by the war effort.

He wove his way through the curtains and found the caves marking the entrance to the labyrinth blocked by piles of jagged rocks, the walls eroded with deep fissures.

Emily's image floated above the wreckage. Her eyes looked empty, haunted. Her hair hung limp around her face. *"So you finally came back. Where's your little honey?"*

"She's dead."

"Sorry, I didn't know."

"She wasn't my little honey."

"I just got a little jealous."

"No time for that now. The labyrinth is collapsing. I have to get you out of here—take your ashes to the mountain."

"Mother isn't there. You said she was with Vaatu."

"It's a long story, but—I hate to tell you this—but Joyce is gone."

"How did—"

At the mention of Joyce's name, hoards of chrome lizards crawled out of the darkness, claws clattering across the rocks. Matt backed away, bracing for an attack. But the lizard's movements were sluggish, tongues lolling between their needle teeth. They moaned as they slithered, a guttural sound that got louder until it shook the ground. Then, in unison, they fell silent, and lay down facing Matt.

"What the hell is going on?" he asked.

"They're grieving."

For a moment, Matt was puzzled. Then the answer came. The lizards were Vaatu's spawn. And their mother? The woman in the red robe. They were mourning the death of their mother. Raava had killed her. An army of vengeful warriors waited at Matt's feet.

"Can you take me to her? Take my ashes up to the mountain?"

"If that's what you want. If you'd rather be with her."

"*I'm not sure—just tell me what happened to my mother.*"

"Raava killed her. She was a spy." Matt walked a few steps closer to Emily's image. The lizards moved aside to let him through. "There might be a way we could be together again," he said, "back in our real lives."

"*Impossible. We're both—ghosts.*"

"There's another way out."

Her image grew larger, projected on the rock wall in front of him. Hate and fear twisted her visage. "*Trust you? The faceless men are gone, the lizards have deserted. I'm all alone in here. I'll be alone forever.*" Her voice rose to a wail. "*I want my mother.*"

"Even after everything she's done? I can relate to that feeling. If I take your ashes up to the mountain there's a good chance I'll never come back, but if that's what you want …"

"*Do you really love me?*"

"I always have."

"*Then save me from this place.*" Her image faded.

The hoard of lizards had grown, covering every inch of the rocky ledge around the Ice Bridge. Matt knelt before the glittering throng and they edged closer, nudging each other with their chrome-plated shoulders.

"I don't know if you can understand me, but I need your help to tear down a mountain."

❧

The Ice Bridge was almost gone, a silver rope gleaming in the starlight. Rivulets of melt water fell in a fairyland cascade toward the river. Matt wrapped his arms around the rope of ice and slid out over the chasm. The lizards, hesitant at first, followed him in single file, a shining parade out over the abyss.

At the Gravity Frontier, the ice disintegrated in a glittering shower down to the river. As the two forces of gravity balanced each other out, Matt floated out into the chasm. The air was cloudy now, filled with the smoke of battle. The dim light barely caught the highlights of the lizards' scales as they soared single file behind Matt. A chrome kite, miles long, snaking toward the Mountain of Ashes.

⁂

The crew from the White Knuckle Roadhouse had parked their bikes and ATVs in a circle around a burning bike tire. They had taken to calling themselves "The Rat Pack." They ate pieces of meat of unknown origin, laughed and jostled each other, ignoring the thud of sticks and stones, the screams of pain, the sounds of battle echoing from the Mountain of Ashes. Their raucous conversation faded as Matt walked into the circle of firelight, boots throwing up a spray of ashes. They stared up at the string of lizards circling single file in the sky above them.

A thin man in a cowboy hat asked, "What the hell is that?"

"Reinforcements." Matt squatted in the sand, accepted a piece of meat on a stick, chewed it, made a face and spat it into the fire.

"Gerbil," Westley said.

Matt motioned for the big man to follow and they walked away from the fire into the deep starlight.

"I notice you didn't bring back your lady love," Westley said.

"She's not interested."

"So you're gonna quit?"

Matt's lip curled but he said nothing.

"I know what love can do to a guy," Westley said.

"I have only one chance to get her out of the labyrinth. I'm going up the mountain. I can't ask you to go with me. Go home."

"I was born at night," Westley said, "but it wasn't last night." He hooked a thumb toward the mountain, a towering black shadow against the stars. "There's a war going on up there. I'm guessing we won't have much of a home to go back to when it's over."

"If things work out the way I planned, you're probably right." Matt shrugged. "Sorry."

"If you succeed with this, a lot of people are going to die."

"Let me ask you something. What they've got in there, in that crystal fun house, and those faceless guys down there in those caves, you call that living?"

Westley stood silent, a pained look on his face.

"Right. Not to mention that everyone we know in the world is food for those two bastards. Forever if nobody stops them."

Westley frowned, hooked his thumbs in his belt. "Maybe you better tell me what it is you have planned."

Matt told him everything, his descent into the labyrinth carrying Emily's ashes, which he now carried caked on his leathers, how her mother had been a spy for Vaatu, infiltrating Raava's conference in the upper world, and how Raava had killed her in retribution. "I went to both camps and told each of them that the other side was planning a huge assault. Neither one took it very well."

"Don't imagine so," Westley said. "What happens now?"

"All the energy in this place is going into the war. Both side's home bases are starting to collapse. The war heats up enough, even the mountain will come down. Vaatu said that might happen. I'm being selfish, but the only way to get Emily back is bring this whole goddamn enterprise down."

"What do you want us to do?"

"Do you remember 'Transactional Analysis'?" Matt asked. "Back in the sixties they had a game called, 'Let's You and Him Fight.'"

Westley fingered his chin. "I don't remember the sixties, or much of anything before the White Knuckle Roadhouse, but I like the sound of that."

"Here's what I want you to do." They huddled, heads together under the stars.

They walked back to the fire and Westley waved to the Rat Pack. "Mount up." He nodded to Matt, patted the ATVs seat. "Hop on."

A broken range of foothills surrounded the Mountain of Ashes. The layers of ash got deeper as Matt and his rag-tag armada approached it. After a few hours ride, the Rat Pack was on foot, their bikes and ATVs mired in the sand. Here, the mountain dominated the landscape, a monstrous grey cone cutting off starlight, reaching beyond human vision.

The lizards followed overhead, trailing Matt, who they seemed to have adopted as their leader. To test his control he waved his arms in a circle and then pointed to his left, the direction of Raava's forces. The lizards swerved left, and disappeared over a crest in the foothills. Matt, Westley, and the rest of the White Knuckle gang climbed the hill and watched the assault.

The lizards dodged and darted around the base of the mountain like fighter planes assaulting a carrier. In an hour they returned, shreds of white fabric still clinging to their teeth. Raava, the god who had killed Joyce, their mother, had a fearsome new enemy at his heels.

Matt and his gang sat on the crest of a hill in the shadow of the Mountain of Ashes, sharpening their knives, checking the loads in their pistols. One man carried a sturdy wooden chair he had hauled in on his ATV. He stroked the legs lovingly. A good chair was a requisite weapon in any decent bar fight. But this bar fight would be different. Matt's instructions had been clear. The Rat Pack would fight under a false flag.

Westley swept off his fedora and addressed his troops. "Our friend, Matt, here is trying to help us poor in-between folks. And now it's our turn to help him. Raava drove poor little Tanya to kill herself. He raped and degraded her—and all of us.

"I'm asking you to make a hell of a sacrifice. This battle could turn out to destroy everything we know. But there may be something better for us afterward."

"Don't give us that crap about a life ever after," one of the men said. "Resting in peace on this mountain. We know that's bullshit."

Matt stood up. "We don't even know if there'll be a mountain after this is over. But anything is better than living forever in a roadhouse, guarding a border for a low-life god."

"'Low-life god.' I like that," Westley said. "Wouldn't have dared to say anything like that a little while ago."

"I told my wife I'm going up to put her ashes on the mountain where she can join her mother's spirit." Matt held out his arms showing the hardened grey coating on the black leather.

"You lied, didn't you?"

"She believes I'm going to sacrifice myself for her—for love. If I don't make it, at least she'll remember me well. But it's a hell of a lot more complicated than that. I don't know if taking her ashes up on the mountain will reunite her with her mom or not, but I'm not going to take that chance." He peeled off his leathers and handed them to Westley.

"You're going to fight the gods in your skivvies?"

"The Greeks did. If everything comes tumbling down, the labyrinth will likely break open."

Westley pulled off his hat, wiped his forehead. "Hell of a long shot."

"It's the only chance I have to get her out."

"What if the gods destroy you first?"

"Then they destroy me and nothing about this world will change. They would both love that. I've caused them a bit of trouble bringing my wife's ashes into the labyrinth. That's why I have to leave you now. I'll only draw fire on you."

"You can't go up there," Westley said.

"I have to. I'm the target. They're both looking for me. I'll draw them toward each other. This skirmishing has probably been going on for centuries. What's different is that the gods themselves are getting into the fight. Up to now they've been directing things from the sidelines."

"Personal, now," Westley said.

"Once they get into it one-on-one I'm betting they'll destroy each other."

"And the mountain comes tumbling down?"

Matt nodded. "And it's up to us to make it worse. Tell anybody you meet that the Ash Man is coming, and he's too smart and too tough to catch. He's outwitted the gods at every turn."

"That's suicide for you."

Matt pulled a cannon ball out of his jacket and chewed it. "The lizards will follow me. They're out to fuck up Raava. That should be a nice diversion."

"Odds are still way against you," Westley said. Mumbles of assent rose from the group.

"That's why I need your help," Matt said. "Whip Vaatu into a frenzy. Insult him at every turn. Think you can handle that?"

The ragged circle of men chuckled. "Eat my shorts," one of them yelled. "Chew my Bermudas."

"Now you're talking."

Chapter Eighteen

Matt trudged up the mountain. Drifting ashes, the remnants of a hundred billion human souls, swirled around his boots. It got colder the higher he climbed. A cloud bank lay thick and opaque above him. The sounds of battle were louder now, attesting to the location of the main battle higher up. The forces were working their way up the mountain. A white-robed figure dropped from the sky and lay twitching on the slope above him. Matt stripped off the soldier's white robe and wrapped it around him, a thin barrier against the cold. The phalanx of chrome lizards swooped down and tore the naked corpse apart.

"Save your energy for the live ones," Matt said.

The lizards withdrew and circled above him.

It was terrifying to reflect on the fact that he would die in what was essentially a giant, miles-high graveyard. The sense of his own mortality overwhelmed him and he recalled his decision, made half-way down the cliff, as he plunged into the labyrinth. He did not want to live without Emily.

Something that had not occurred to him: what if he left his own ashes up here on the mountain? Would he reunite with Emily in some kind of peaceful afterlife? It didn't, as he stood looking up at the mountain, seem very likely. He must get them both out of this place, back across the river and back to reality. For this was not reality, this was a twisted fever dream where strange creatures and false gods raged at each other across a surreal landscape.

He must take this mad construction down, force its denizens to destroy themselves, and then somehow climb out of the rubble—with Emily—and go back to their lives, without the influence of Vaatu or Raava.

What force had thrown Vaatu's girlfriend into Matt's happy suburban life? And what force had prompted Joyce's arc toward justice at the end? It was almost enough to make you laugh—the classic evil mother-in-law joke. But this was no joke. Her hideous children, the chrome spawn of an evil god, had broken ranks and now hovered above his head, waiting to do battle with Raava.

Raava supposedly represented goodness and light, but was, in fact, venal and vengeful. A god who captured women, made them sex slaves, and had driven Tanya to kill herself.

Matt felt bad that he had deceived Emily, but there was no choice if he were to get her out of the labyrinth— with him. He had told her he was willing to go up on the mountain, sacrifice himself in order to reunite her with her mother. She had agreed with that, apparently loving her mother more than him. And she would have been right, if he had still been the self-centered creep he had been in his life above in the "real" world. But he was changed now, and all his energy was channeled to winning Emily back. He had seen what a cold, empty world it was without her.

He had lied to Emily. He had no intention of leaving her ashes on the mountain. If he did she might stay forever with her mother—and he, if his ashes were there also—would exist beside them for all eternity. Just thinking about it made his skin crawl. He would take Emily with him and get out of here somehow, across the river.

He carried no cannonballs with him. This was not the time to be invisible; it was a time for confrontation. How could a mere mortal ever expect to win such a battle? Matt's answer was simple: whip both sides into such a frenzy they destroyed each other and forgot about him. His plan required that every element worked perfectly. First, he knew that both gods hungered to destroy him. He would be the bait, taunting them—forcing them to crash head on and, with luck, bring the mountain down.

Westley and his Rat Pack would keep harassing both sides, nipping at their heels, distracting them with fake attacks. Several of the denizens of the White Knuckle Roadhouse slogged up the mountain to Matt's left chanting as they climbed, "Raava sucks." Another band on the right chanted, "Vaatu sucks." Juvenile and stupid, perhaps, but given the childish, thin-skinned nature of the two gods, it surely would be effective.

A long line of faceless men materialized out of the clouds and stomped toward Westley's pro-Raava crowd. Clubs and fists flew, pistol shots echoed across the mountain and a row of faceless men fell, head-down, in the ashes. A faceless warrior's club connected with the tall cowboy in the leather vest, crushing his Stetson. He spun in a lazy circle and fell. Two of his cohorts carried him back down the mountain.

One of Westley's men pointed toward a horde of decaying corpses staggering toward them, arms outstretched. He emptied his pistol into the fetid mass with no effect.

"I don't fuck with no zombies." He threw down his pistol and ran down the mountain, stumbled and fell in the ashes. They were on him in a hundred yards.

Raava's white-robed air force dived in, raining stones down on The Rat Pack. Several of Westley's gang picked up the stones and hurled them back, knocking white-robed fighters out of the sky. A shotgun boomed, cutting a hole in the cloud of aerial attackers. The sky cleared as the flying army, realizing their vulnerability, flew away in retreat to report back to their generals. Their flanks were being attacked.

The Rat Pack's assault, like a well-executed quarterback sneak, opened up the mountainside ahead of Matt. He climbed faster, energized by the victory. Soon he was in the clouds. No way to tell how far away the summit lay. His legs burned with the effort; his breath threw white puffs into the now-frigid air.

He finally broke free of the clouds into the freezing air. The sky above him was crowded with flailing bodies, a reenactment of the Game he had seen in Raava's glass and crystal realm.

The bodies piled up as he climbed. He pawed his way through the tangle, a mixture of white robed and faceless corpses. A scattering of the monsters who had guarded the Ice Bridge lay strewn amid the carnage. A saber-toothed rat with florescent red fur, head impaled on a stick, sat among the chopped-up pieces of a winged snake. A purple alligator lay sprawled on its back, a white stone buried in its stomach.

And there amid the carnage, black-lacquered tank coated with ashes, sat the Harley.

Matt raised his fist in jubilation. All good bikes went to heaven. He straddled the beast and jabbed the starter button. Again.

Again.

The big bike was dead.

"Air filter."

Matt turned at the sound of Westley's voice.

The big man pulled off the bike's air filter. "Packed with dust. No way to clean that baby up here."

"What happens if I ride without it?"

"Suck dirt into the throttle body. Destroy the engine."

The mountain shook, thunderous footsteps rumbled up the left side. The lizards circling above began a frantic chattering and flew away around the back side.

"What the hell's gotten into them?" Wesley asked.

"Raava's coming. Looks like the general is finally getting into the fight." Matt climbed on the Harley.

"You start that bike and the engine's screwed."

"This old bike has been screwed before, a lot worse than this." Matt jabbed the throttle. The bike roared to life. He bipped the engine, smiled at the sound.

Westley said, "Where's the other guy?"

Matt threw his head back and shouted over the Harley's rumble, "Vaatu probably hasn't got the *balls*."

Thunderous foot falls shook the ground on Vaatu's side of the mountain.

Westley took off his black leather coat and handed it to Matt. "It might get a little chilly up there in your skivvies."

Matt slipped it on over this tee-shirt. "Thanks."

"Take care, *Mon Capitaine*."

Matt leaned forward over the handlebars and gunned the bike up the mountain, trailing a plume of ash. The Rat Pack picked up the chant: "Vaatu got no *balls*."

Chapter Nineteen

Emily's spirit hovered in the deserted labyrinth, fighting panic. The labyrinth was coming apart. The faceless men no longer roamed the corridors; the chrome lizard den into which she had lured Matt was an empty trench. Passageways had caved in, choked with broken stone. The seething chamber of molten lava had cooled to a stiff black mass. Even the pit filled with rotting cadavers where Matt had fallen was empty now. Where had those poor souls—or non-souls—gone? But still the river ran sparkling and cool, bathed in a blue light of its own making. By its banks lay her funeral urn, washed clean of all her ashes. The silver glowed faintly in the water's luminance.

This was where it all began, the moment Matt brought her ashes into the labyrinth. She barely understood the workings of this grim, dark place but it was evident that her ashes being introduced here was a strange anomaly. A woman, crushed to death in a car wreck was suddenly alive—or some version of alive. She had been overjoyed at being given another chance to experience the world, even this bleak version of it.

Then Matt showed up. Her last vision of him had been his tear-stained face looking down as she lay dying. Then blackness, then her awakening to see him struggling with a twisted mass of corpses, reaching for her funeral urn. The moment her ashes flew free and covered his body, she knew she must direct him through the maze. She saw a path ahead, but her feelings were mixed. Her last thought had been that he had driven her to her death with his cheating. She had fled from him in fear and rage, raced into a cemetery and crashed.

Something wasn't right about that moment, but the details were fuzzy. Whatever had happened, she was sure Matt was to blame. She had been sent back—to punish him, sending him into the chrome lizard's den, deserting him in the darkness, watching him disintegrate mentally, making him feel torture as she had felt it.

She got him to the Ice Bridge and he had disappeared, only to show up later with some babe in a red nightie. At that memory, she felt her rage against him rise. But now the dilemma: he had gone to free her from this place, put her on the Mountain of Ashes with her mother. He had gone to die—but now, she wanted him to live, to come and save her. She had been stubborn and foolish.

She had heard her mother's voice inside her head demanding she lead Matt out to the Ice Bridge. Joyce had told her of the mountain and given her a clear message. Her ashes must go there. And Matt must carry them, transporting them on his motorcycle leathers. Going onto the mountain would be the end of Matt, but she hated the bastard, anyway, didn't she? At that moment she had heartily agreed.

Now she was not so sure. She remembered their last conversation:

"Do you really love me?"

"I always have."

Fifteen years of marriage had to count for something. He had always surprised her, made her laugh. Once, as they walked along a moonlit beach in Bodega Bay he declared himself an authority on Glen Campbell and broke into "Rhinestone Cowboy." Who knew he could sing?

What trials had he gone through after he disappeared down the Ice Bridge? Had she sent him into oblivion? The whole underworld order had been turned on its head. Something terrible was happening, much bigger than she and Matt. The labyrinth was collapsing, taking her down with it, trapping her forever in solitary darkness.

She trembled at the thought.

❧

Matt danced the bike up the mountain, far above the clouds now, his only goal to climb as far as he could before the Harley choked to death on the ashes. A mass of clouds hung over it sending out flashes of lightning.

A blizzard enveloped Matt, obscuring the peak. The bike's back tire spun in the slurry of ash and snow. Matt clung to the handlebars, fighting for control. His coat was stiff with ice, his fingers frozen to the handlebars. The Harley was slowing down. Every fiber of his being screamed at him to quit. He forced his mind to thoughts of Emily. Her face shimmered before him against a curtain of snow. He opened the throttle.

The mountainside was nearly vertical. The engine screamed; the bike wobbled and bounced up the slope, front wheel in the air. Then he was on top. Drifting ashes of newly-arrived souls settled around him. The bike sank tank-deep, sputtered and died.

A few cannon balls floated toward Matt, fizzled into the snow and faded out. The battle was draining energy from the mountain.

Raava loomed against the sky, taller than a skyscraper now. His Viking helmet touched the clouds. Lighting crackled between the horns. He waved his sword, cursing the squadrons of chrome lizards dive-bombing him. He pointed the sword at Matt, eyes cold and dead. "Ash Man."

Matt looked at the figure towering above him. He saw something besides vanity and rage in the false god's face. Despair. Surrender to the inevitable conclusion that he would never get off this mountain alive.

Vaatu's gleaming chrome visage appeared over the crest of the mountain. "He's mine." His steel-taloned hands, now the size of steam shovels, reached for Matt.

The wind from Raava's sword swirled the ashes as it flashed over Matt's head and struck Vaatu's talons away.

"You're slow, clown," Raava said.

The brass rivets on Vaatu's bandoleers glowed dull gold, rising and falling as the giant breathed. Puffs of his breath floated up toward the clouds. "You call me a clown? That slur will be avenged."

A condescending smile twisted Raava's lips. "A clown and weakling. Your forces are falling. You reign is over." He pounded the chain mail taut across his monstrous chest. "All of this is *mine*." His arm swept the horizon.

Vaatu leaped onto the plateau, feet wide apart, talons extended. His voice was an evil hiss: "Mine!" The needle-toothed jaws flashed out, clamped on Raava's sword hand. Raava howled and stepped back. Vaatu shook his jaws, tearing at Raava's arm like a dog.

Raava brought a fist down on Vaatu's head. The giant fell to his knees dazed. Raava raised his sword, slashed Vaatu's shoulder, nearly severing his arm. Vaatu snaked his good arm around Raava's ankle, yanked him off his feet. The two gods squirmed in the ashes, looking for an opening. Vaatu snagged his claws in Raava's chain mail, ripped it open, exposing Raava's belly.

Raava rolled away from the slashing claws, and whipped a backhand sword strike, severing Vaatu's leather bandoliers. They tangled around his ankles and he struggled to free himself. Raava's sword flew from his hand and banged off the Harley's tank, missing Matt's head by an inch. It came to rest on the edge of the crater, hilt pointed downhill. The blade, shiny and polished, was two feet wide and the height of two men.

Vaatu grabbed Raava in a bear hug from behind, claws digging into the exposed flesh. Raava sunk his teeth into Vaatu's wounded arm, ripped out a chunk of flesh. Vaatu's eyes rolled back. He shook it off and bit deeply into Raava's neck. Raava lashed out with a steel boot, finding a target on Vaatu's chrome-scaled back, breaking ribs. A red-tinted mush of snow and ashes churned around them as they bit and clawed each other. Their screams rose to a deafening crescendo.

Thunder boomed, lightning struck the ground all around them. The gods halted their mortal combat and stared at each other, still locked in their savage embrace. The strikes fused the ashes into sheets of gray glass.

The rumble of thunder had come not from the clouds but from within the mountain. The snow had stopped, the sky hung low. They struggled to their feet glowering at each other, panting, exhausted. Like punctured balloons, both combatants shrank—down to human scale. Matt ran across the ice and hit Raava with a running tackle. He locked his hands around the god's throat and pounded his head against the ice until Raava collapsed, unconscious.

❧

A bright white light flashed overhead. A hologram hovered in the sky: The walls of Raava's glass and crystal world cracked. Sparkling pieces fell off into the sea, tearing down great crystal sheets as they fell. Finally the last pieces tumbled down and sank beneath the waters.

⁃

Vaatu grabbed Matt's coat with his steel talons and pulled him to his feet.

As Matt struggled, helpless in the god's grasp, Joyce's words came back. He shouted, "Don't get too excited, you'll piss yourself like a puppy." He pointed at Vaatu's crotch.

Vaatu glanced down. A yellow stream trickled down his chrome pants leg. His body shook. He unleashed an unearthly howl as he shrank, morphing into the form of Larry Unger.

The two men stood eye-to-eye. Larry took off his glasses, polished them on the tail of his shirt. "She told you, didn't she?"

"She did. Guess she didn't like being used as your baby machine. But, your ego, your vanity, I figured that out for myself." Matt feinted with his left hand, slammed an uppercut into Larry Unger's jaw, something he had yearned to do for twenty-five years.

Larry toppled across Raava's unconscious form. Matt stared down at his body. In the end, Joyce had done the right thing. That realization freed something in his chest. The old, bitter hatred dissolved, lifted and melted away.

A crack snaked toward them across the ice and the mountain began to shake. Matt jumped back. The crack became a yawning crevasse. Blackness hid its true depth.

Raava and Vaatu slid into the crevasse and disappeared.

A roaring wind swept across the plateau, sending a choking cloud of ashes up from the slopes below. The mountain began to tremble like a dying beast. The whole thing was coming down.

Matt grabbed the hilt of Raava's giant sword, teetering on the edge of the cliff. He folded Westley's black leather coat over the blade like a saddle and threw himself on. He pushed off with his foot, slid over the edge and down the wall of ash, riding the sword.

He caught air several times, slashing through the deserted battlefield, knocking aside faceless corpses and white-robed warriors. He ducked his head and held his breath to avoid the blinding slipstream of ashes from the sword's hilt. No sign of the Rat Pack.

The wind became a hurricane, almost pushing him to a standstill. He managed a quick glance over his shoulder. The mountain was half its former height, a swirling tornado of ashes sweeping upward toward the stars. The mountain was blowing away. Matt clung to the hilt, squinting against the flying ash. The sword slowed, crossing ashen foothills, and finally ground to a standstill at the edge of the desert.

Dead silence. Then the faint crunch of boots from the other side of a dune. Matt stood up to face this new aggressor, armed with a powerful weapon he couldn't lift.

Westley and two men in cowboy hats, bodies bent into the wind, topped the dune and limped toward him. Westley, fedora jammed down over a crown of bandages, a pack slung over his shoulder, held a small white dog in his arms. "Some of the boys wanted to barbecue him, but I thought he looked too cute." He passed Baxter to Matt.

The dog stared up at him, tail wagging. "Who's a good boy?" The wagging stopped. "You hate condescending language, don't you, Baxter?" The dog cocked his head as if he understood. Matt set him down and he scampered off.

Westley sat in the sand, massaging his left leg.

"You ok?" Matt shouted over the wind.

"Busted something. Just glad to be alive." He got halfway to his feet, winced and sat back down. "There's only the three of us left. This is Bronco, and this tall drink of water is Big Frank." Both men tipped their Stetsons. "We took a heck of a lot of them with us, though."

"Sorry for your loss. You're all brave men." Matt shook their hands.

Bronco said, "We knew what we signed up for."

"What the hell happened up there?" Westley asked.

"Raava and Vaatu are gone, the mountain's coming down, the labyrinth is collapsing. Raava's glass palace crashed into the ocean."

"Nothing left for us to guard." Westley shrugged. "Not that we did that great a job." He explained how he had lost ten of his men in a last desperate assault that had forced the Rat Pack to retreat down the mountain. "They went crazy, threw their sticks at us, tore us up with those damn white rocks," he said. "They knew the end was coming."

"The end is coming," Matt said, "but it's not here yet, not until I get Emily out of the labyrinth."

"How's that gonna happen? You said it's collapsing."

"I have to try. There was a portal up by the Raavacon conference site. Maybe it's still open."

Westley reached in his pack and pulled out Matt's ash-crusted leathers. "You'll need these."

Chapter Twenty

Matt rigged a travois for Westley behind the one functioning motorcycle, using sticks the faceless men had dropped. Bronco and Big Frank climbed on the bike, Matt walked alongside. Baxter trotted ahead across the timeless landscape, sniffing the ground.

Exhausted, they finally reached the spot where Tonto's guard shack had stood. Broken pieces lay scattered on the sand, mixed with the charred remains of the giant yucca. Matt kicked a broken board and cursed. A small creature flitted away across the sand. Baxter gave chase.

Westley sat up on his makeshift stretcher and yawned. Matt knelt beside him. "How's the leg?" he said.

"Okay, long as I don't move. My head hurts like hell though, like when you clocked me down at the White Knuckle. Don't think I can make it too much farther." Bronco and Big Frank climbed off the bike and went to relieve themselves on the sand.

Matt squeezed the big man's shoulder. "Rest easy."

He climbed a narrow ridge nearby and called to Baxter. Frenzied barking erupted over the hill. Matt went to investigate. Baxter had cornered some small rodent. He growled, feet braced, as Matt approached. "Don't worry boy, I won't steal your prey."

A flash of light caught Matt's eye and he stepped closer. Baxter's "prey" was a baby chrome lizard. The creature crouched in the sagebrush baring his tiny steel teeth.

"Stay, Baxter. Even the little ones will fuck you up." Baxter whimpered, but backed away. Matt knelt down and whispered, "Take it easy, little guy. We were on the same side a little while ago." The lizard froze, eyes flitting across the giant creature looming over him. Matt held out an ash-covered sleeve. The lizard crept closer, touched its metallic snout to the leather. Matt picked him up. It nuzzled against him like a puppy. Its primal instinct had been awakened by the smell of Emily's ashes on his coat. Its half-sister's ashes.

If there was a creature on earth who knew the way back to Emily, this tiny lizard was it. Matt set him down on the sand. Baxter crept forward. "Sit." Baxter sat. The lizard had grown, nearly a foot long now, a teenager in lizard years. It swiveled its head to look at Matt.

"Find her."

The lizard skittered away and Matt followed at a slow trot, Baxter at his heels. On the other side of the ridge the lizard found a faint path that looked familiar. A cliff fell away on the left and Matt caught the faint sound of rushing water. Familiar landmarks appeared: a cluster of rocks, a sharp rise in the sand. It was the path he had ridden on the Harley. The lizard followed the faint tire track. That made perfect sense. Matt had carried her funeral urn along this path. Then the lizard veered off toward the cliff and Matt felt the chill of fear. He knew where he was going.

The lizard stopped at the cliff's edge and looked down, as if contemplating the distance of his fall. He looked back at Matt. *Your choice.*

Matt crept forward and peeked over the edge. Plumes of white water crashed over the rocks at the bottom of the canyon. Mist nurtured a fringe of vegetation along the bank. A beautiful scene, one Matt hadn't noticed when he rode his Harley over the edge. He had been certain then that he was going to die. There would be no hesitation now. Live or die, he was going over. He stepped out onto a rock ledge and looked up, taking in the sky. Baxter whined, pawed at Matt's pants leg. He patted the animal's head and stepped off into the air. The lizard dove after him.

Alone on the edge of the cliff, Baxter howled at the distant stars.

☙

As the dog ran back to the Rat Pack, the sky lightened, the stars faded, and the sun rose through the haze beyond the mountain. The last of the ashes spiraled away and disappeared against the brightening sky. The ordinary sounds of the desert returned: the chirping of birds, the scuttling of small animals through sagebrush, the distant howl of a coyote.

A herd of Longhorn steers grazed in the sagebrush, buzzards sailed above them in the hard blue sky. Baxter ran behind, barking.

Bronco saw the herd and he reached automatically for his rope. But his saddle and his horse had long since disappeared.

"That's prime beef down there," Big Frank said.

Bronco said, "We didn't always eat gerbils, did we?"

"I think my memory is coming back," Westley scratched his chin, "Must have been that bump on my head." He held his fedora over his heart. "I sure remember steaks."

"And ribs," Bronco said.

Westley shook his head. "Pretty soon this is gonna be just a plain old desert. Matt better hurry before the magic's gone."

The lizard lay beside Matt on a rocky ledge beside the river, his claws shaking, tongue flickering in and out. He had overcome his aversion to water, but the effort had cost him. The pink light from his neon tongue was fading, but Matt recognized the ledge and the rushing water just beyond. The corpse-filled pit lay only a few steps away, the place he had first encountered Emily's spirit.

Matt crept toward the pit, guided only by the faint light from the lizard's tongue. The lizard crawled beside him, his movements slow, jerky, a creature in pain.

"Hang on. We'll find her." They reached the edge of the pit and peered over. Though the light was faint, it was obvious the pit was empty, its soulless denizens gone to fight for a lost cause.

Ahead somewhere in the darkness lay the endless alkaline plane where he had first seen the mysterious light (had it been the Harley's headlight?) and met the faceless men on their hopeless journey into oblivion. They too had gone to give their lives to a higher power, though they'd probably had no choice. Now Emily was the only creature, besides himself, left in the collapsing labyrinth. Somewhere out there her spirit roamed, alone. Terrified.

The lizard turned its head, responding to some sound Matt couldn't hear. It slithered into the pit. Matt followed the faint pink light moving across the bottom and up the other side. The lizard crouched on the far edge of the pit. The pit was at least thirty feet across, too far to jump. No way to climb the sheer rock walls. "Can't make it," Matt said. He cried with frustration. He had come so far. "Emily, where are you?"

•

The cavern lay in total darkness. Emily felt a *presence* surrounding her. She wrapped her arms around her shoulders, shaking with fear. A strange sensation hit her:

she could feel her hands gripping her shoulders. She wiggled her toes, felt the coolness of the rock beneath her feet. The sharp edges of the boulder she sat on hurt her backside. Feeling had been restored to her body. Why now, when the labyrinth was dying around her? It only meant she would experience with all her senses, the torture of being buried alive. Her mouth opened in a silent scream.

The lizard jerked his head again, and this time Matt heard Emily's scream in his head.

The lizard darted away leaving Matt in darkness.

"Emily?"

"Matt, this lizard thing is looking at me."

"He won't hurt you; he led me to you." Not the time to tell her she was the creature's half-sister.

Matt heard the waterfall to the left and remembered how he had set down Emily's urn and gone to drink from it. Later he found drinking the water had given him a remarkable power: he could breathe underwater.

"Stay where you are, I'm coming."

He crawled back to the rock ledge where the river had left him, stood up beside the fast-running water and dived in headfirst.

Chapter Twenty-one

The lizard was the first to notice Matt's head bobbing in the pool beneath the waterfall. Matt's arms chopped the water as he paddled toward the bank. The lizard chirped and ran toward the water. Emily stumbled after him, still unsure of her footing.

Matt climbed out of the water and shook the water off his leathers. He stared at her as she approached, her body pale, translucent in the dim light. "You're—I can see all of you."

"You came back. I prayed you would." Her regular voice, not the one in his head. Emily was back from the spirit world.

"Come here." He reached for her. His arms circled empty space. Then slowly he felt the familiar contours of her body moving against him. She moaned softly, a familiar, stimulating sound. He reacted instantly, pulling her closer. They kissed, a slow passionate joining that grew into a symphony of exploring lips and tongues. He ran his hands down her back, over the silk fabric of her blouse, the one she had worn when she died.

She gasped. "Matt, I feel you touching me. It feels wonderful." He held her tighter and they kissed again.

The chrome lizard chittered wildly and limped in a circle around them. The little reptile froze, head cocked, listening. The sound, subsonic at first, became an ominous rumble felt in the bones, rolling up from the bowels of the labyrinth. A fissure opened on the bank of the river and water flooded out, moving toward them.

Emily's voice trembled. "Are we going to die?"

"Not today. There may be a way out of this place."

"*May* be? You don't *know*?"

"I came back for you, that's all I was thinking about. Excuse the hell out of me for loving you."

"I'm sorry." She brushed his lips with a finger. "You used to tell me that all the time."

Matt gripped her shoulders and held her at arm's length. "I love you and I'm offering you a chance to go with me, back to what we have been calling the 'real world.'" He studied her face in the flickering light. "If that's what you want."

"Matt, I …"

"Just tell me. Is that what you want?"

"Yes, that's what I want. But how is that even possible? Everything is collapsing."

"You'll just have to trust me." He pulled her against him. Another lingering kiss.

The lizard limped away across the alkaline flat, chittering madly. Matt and Emily followed, dodging fissures snaking across the floor. Cracks opened across the ceiling, flooding the chamber with soft gray light. Matt felt rain on his face.

The lizard veered away into a cavern. They followed, guided only by the fading light of the lizard's neon tongue. The walls shook and chunks of rock fell around them. After what seemed like forever, the lizard led them to an opening in the wall. The river raced beside it, then disappeared into the rocks. It was the spot where he'd dived in, carrying Tanya in her red negligee on his back. The starlight that had filled this chamber had been replaced by gray daylight, streaming through a crack in the rocks above them. Soft rain pattered on the rocks.

They lay down, exhausted. The lizard crawled up beside them and curled into a ball.

"What's the matter with him?" she asked.

"Metal parts don't work well in water."

"Does he know he's out in the rain?

"I think he just wants to be where you are."

"Why me?" she asked.

"All the lizards are Vaatu's spawn."

"And my mother was his … Are you trying to tell me—"

"This little guy is your half-brother. That's why he led me to you."

"I can't think about that."

"I didn't want to tell you," Matt said.

She patted the little creature. He wiggled, then lay still. "My little brother? He's kind of cute, actually."

"He's dying, Emily, everything is dying. The mountain is gone, your mother is gone. Raava and Vaatu are gone."

"You better tell me what the hell happened."

As they sat by the river, heads together, he told her about his trek across the desert, the fight in the White Knuckle Roadhouse, how the Rat Pack had become his allies. He told of his journey to Raava's glass and crystal kingdom, his confrontation with Vaatu and the final, terrible battle on the Mountain of Ashes.

"You lied to me," she said. "You never meant to take my ashes back to the mountain, to let me rest with my mother."

"There is no mountain. Joyce is somewhere out among the stars now. I didn't know that's how things would turn out."

"But you suspected …"

"If I hadn't been able to put the two gods at each other's throats, and the mountain hadn't come down, I would have just dropped your ashes on the mountain and let myself be destroyed. You and your mother would have been together forever. That's not an option anymore. You're stuck with me."

"And we're stuck in this place, with a dying lizard."

"We're going to get out of here, together, if you—"

The cracks in the wall widened and water poured down, draining back into the river.

"We'll drown," Emily said.

"Remember when I jumped in the water with Tanya?"

"I remember you telling me something about being able to breathe underwater."

"Tanya told me that drinking from the headwaters of the river gave me some kind of power."

"You mean it's true?"

"It's how I snuck past Vaatu."

"You're still full of surprises."

"Want to hear a little Glen Campbell?" Matt asked

"Maybe later." The rumble from below grew louder, the walls shook sending small boulders into the water. "If there is a later."

"Now, or never," Matt said.

He slipped into the water and lay face down. Emily climbed on his back, locked her arms around his neck. Together, they went over the falls.

❧

The world was upside down, topsy-turvy, a watery pinball machine. Emily held her breath as they careened into a tunnel, fought panic in the blackness. Just before her reflexes forced her to breathe, they popped out into an open channel and she turned her head to the side, breathing like a swimmer gasping for air. Matt held his arms out in a "Superman" pose, slicing through the water with his head underneath. They plunged down a long series of rapids. The canyon walls were falling apart around them, crashing into the river. Emily's grip was getting weaker, her arms numb from holding onto Matt's neck.

But the light was gradually growing stronger and the current was slowing. As the river widened, she could see a slice of the sky above, gray and foreboding. Lightning flashed and as the spray diminished she could feel the rain on her face, see it puckering the surface of the water around her. The water was shallower, translucent green over gravel. Matt's head was still underwater. Emily loosened her grip, flexed her arms to get circulation back. The water was less than a foot deep now, the current scarcely moving. Emily rolled off Matt's back and sat up. He slipped his arm around her shoulder. "Are you okay?"

"Where are we?"

The horizon lay flat before them. The Mountain of Ashes was gone. The river was now a thin trickle across the sand. Matt helped her to her feet. "This desert was kind of a no-man's land between Ravva and Vaatu's worlds. Those worlds are gone and I'm not sure what this place is now." They climbed onto the bank. A mottled carpet of flowers, pink, yellow and blue lay at their feet.

"Beautiful," she said. "Belly flowers,"

"Right, you have to lie on your belly to see them."

"Like down in Death Valley."

"Where the scorpion crawled up your—" Matt said.

They laughed at the shared memory. They were finishing each other's thoughts now, like when they first met. It felt good.

She lay down, oblivious to the rain on her back, sniffed a tiny cluster of blue flowers. "Smells like strawberries," she said.

He lay beside her. He smiled. "Strawberries."

They lay that way together for a long time. Small birds gathered in the branches of a Joshua tree, seeking shelter. "I love you," she said. "I'm sorry for being so selfish."

"I'm sorry for lying to you. I guess I did it because I'm selfish, too. I just wanted you for myself."

"We've always had our lowest moments together, but we've always come out on the other side."

"We're not on the other side yet," Matt said.

"As the saying goes, 'Things always work out in the end. And if they don't work out, it's not the end.'" An apologetic shrug. "My mother used to say that."

"Of course she did."

A barbed wire fence stretched alongside the river. A lone figure wearing a black leather coat limped slowly toward them across the endless expanse of sand. Rain dripped off his fedora, plastering wisps of white hair across his forehead. Westley.

He tipped his hat when Matt made the introductions. "This is Emily," Matt said.

Her blouse, made transparent by the water, clung to her. She crossed her arms over her chest and nodded at the big man,

"After the mountain was gone, the sun came out," Westley said. "The ashes got swept up in the wind. Then it clouded up and started to rain. Ordinary rain like this." He held out his palm. "Not that acid stuff."

"And the ashes came back down?"

Westley nodded. "Flowers started to grow, we heard the coyotes again, even saw a herd of cattle."

"The desert came back to life."

Westley said, "This desert used to be a magical place, but it was unnatural magic. The magic is natural now. Sweet air, cool water, birds, flowers. This is the way I remember it."

Matt said, "The way it should be."

The rain stopped, the clouds drifted away toward the horizon.

"We had a hell of a life out here. Only the three of us left, but by damn we're still cowboys. We've been following a herd for a couple of days now. They headed that way. Likely looking for water."

"The river's down to a trickle, "Matt said.

"It disappears into the sand about a mile down that way."

"Disappears? We have to cross it to get back to the real world."

"That's what they say, but nobody *knows*."

Emily said, "If the river is gone, where are we supposed to cross?"

"I'd go that way; follow the herd. They smell the water. Has to come back up somewhere. It's just not part of *this* place anymore," Westley said. "Better get moving, it's gonna be dark soon. I'll be traveling that way too, but the boys and I will be moving a little slower. So we might not see you again." He tipped his hat. "Ma'am." He and Matt shook hands. "I wish you luck, but if you don't make it, be on the lookout for our campfire. We'll cook up a steak for you."

Matt and Emily trekked across the sand under the setting sun, following the faint trace of the dry riverbed. Westley followed until his figure was lost in the gathering twilight. Emily shivered in the darkness. They came to a barbed wire fence. A rusted sign hung from the wire. "Restricted Area."

Matt raised the top strand to help Emily through.

"You people can't read?" A bearded man carrying a long pole stepped out of the gathering gloom.

A black robe cloaked his body, its cowl hid his face. He swung the pole across his chest. "There's no place for you here."

"We're looking to cross the river."

"You don't want to get near the river."

A faint reddish glow spread across the sand behind him, a distant expanse of water sparkled in the reddish light. A boat rested on the shore. Figures climbed out and trudged toward the light. A herd of longhorns grazed beside the water.

"What is this place?" Emily asked.

"Not a place you want to be," the man said.

"We have to get to the river—get across the river."

"That's never happened."

"We came down the river through the labyrinth."

"That's never happened either, unless—" The old man stepped closer, peered over the fence. "You're the one who brought the mountain down. You're the Ash Man."

"How much is passage on your boat?"

The cloaked man's lip curled into what might have been a smile. "Can't really say. Don't get that many round trips."

As twilight deepened, the glow behind the old man resolved itself into a cave filled with fire, set into a wall of black stone. A long line of human forms shuffled toward the entrance.

Matt took an involuntary step back. "Is that … ?"

"It's whatever you believe it is." The old man bowed at the waist, straightened and held out his hand. "Charon. Bob Charon."

"You don't have to bow to me," Matt said.

"You drank from the headwaters and now you are here at the very end. No one has made that journey before. I honor your incredible voyage, but I'm sorry, I cannot let you go farther." He planted his pole in the sand. "Please excuse me, I have to pick up more passengers."

"No, wait. What's the fare? I'll pay anything."

"Anything? What if I told you I could only take one of you?"

Matt and Emily pointed at each other. "Take—"

The old man smiled and held up his hand. "Love is *one* thing that will free you from this place. You've passed the first test."

"What's the second test?" Emily asked.

"One of you will likely fail."

The couple leaned closer, holding hands as Charon talked. When he finished, they looked at each other and nodded.

"We best hurry." Charon balanced his pole across his shoulder. "This boat waits for no one."

❧

A gargoyle figurehead decorated the prow of the old man's boat. "Ra," in flowing script was carved in the weathered wood. Matt sat in the bow as Charon poled across the black water. The shore was visible now. A crowd of people waited amidst clusters of marsh grass and rotted stumps. Rotted suits, mud-stained gowns. Burial clothes.

Matt fought an almost overwhelming urge to look back at Emily standing on the far bank. He tensed his neck muscles, gripped the gunwales and forced his gaze forward as the boat approached the bank.

Charon said, "I see you've read your mythology."

The boat slid through the reeds onto the bank. Matt climbed out and stood, back turned to the river. Charon smiled again. "You can turn around."

Matt turned. Emily stood in the boat. He took her hand and helped her out. They kissed. He took off his jacket and slipped it around her shoulders.

On the far shore, a campfire glowed against the sky. A group of men sat around it, eating chunks of roasted meat impaled on their hunting knives. One of them, a newcomer, picked up a guitar. His soulful tenor echoed across the water: "The Wichita Lineman."

ABOUT THE AUTHOR

John is the author of seven novels and numerous shorter non-fiction works. He has conducted writing workshops, classes and seminars around the country for the past 20 years; his sensitive and insightful critiques have inspired hundreds of writers. His classes on the novel, short stories, essays and magazine writing have given many students a stepping stone to publication. Currently, John is editing a book-length collection of essays by Northwest writers.

johnreedbooks.com

Complete Rulebook
&
Labyrinth of Souls Tarot Deck
Available at
matthewlowes.com/games

Labyrinth of Souls Fiction
Coming Soon
Bayou's Lament by Cheryl Owen-Wilson
Perilous by Cynthia Coate-Ray
Exhumation of the Divine by Pamela Jean Herber
... and more to come!
information at
shadowspinnerspress.com